BY KEAN SOO

STONE ARCH BOOKS

a capstone imprint

March Grand Prix
published by Stone Arch Books,
a Capstone Imprint
1710 Roe Crest Drive
North Mankato, Minnesota 56003
www.capstonepub.com

Text Copyright © Kean Soo 2015.
Illustration Copyright © Kean Soo 2015.

All rights reserved. No part of this publication
may be reproduced in whole or in part, or
stored in a retrieval system, or transmitted in any
form or by any means, electronic, mechanical,
photocopying, recording, or otherwise, without
written permission of the publisher.

Cataloging-in-Publication Data is available on
the Library of Congress website.

ISBN: 978-1-4342-9640-5 (library hardcover)
ISBN: 978-1-4342-9643-6 (paperback)
ISBN: 978-1-4965-0185-1 (eBook)

Summary: March Hare's first race for Tuttle
Racing is the infamous Desert Rally. March
and his GT Superturbo must endure extreme
conditions, deadly competitors, and an
unexpected co-driver who has her own agenda!

Printed in the United States of America
in North Mankato, Minnesota.
012016   009422R

KEAN SOO
MARCH GRAND PRIX

THE BAKER'S RUN

To Juni,

For providing the first spark.

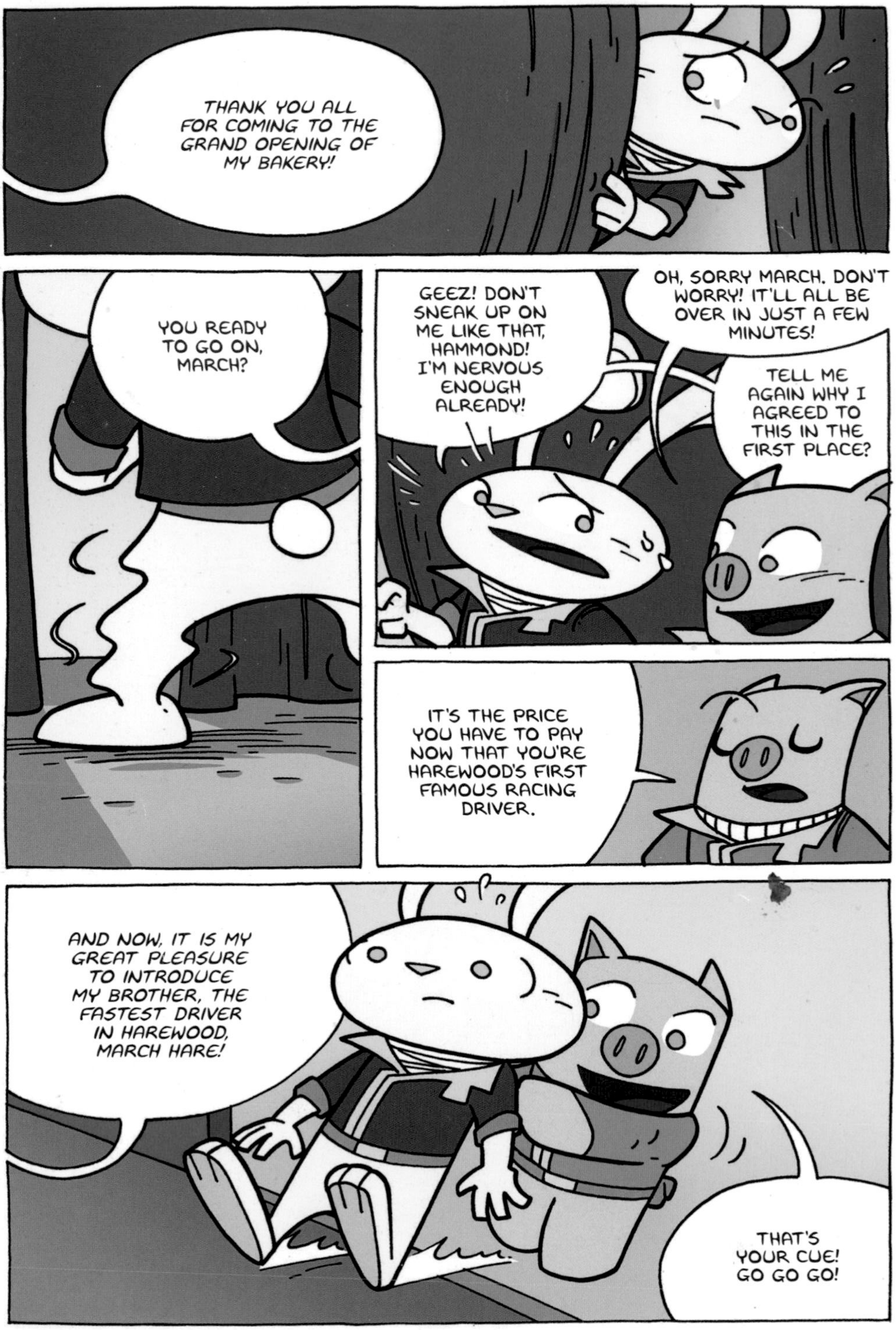
THANK YOU ALL FOR COMING TO THE GRAND OPENING OF MY BAKERY!
YOU READY TO GO ON, MARCH?
GEEZ! DON'T SNEAK UP ON ME LIKE THAT, HAMMOND! I'M NERVOUS ENOUGH ALREADY!
OH, SORRY MARCH. DON'T WORRY! IT'LL ALL BE OVER IN JUST A FEW MINUTES!
TELL ME AGAIN WHY I AGREED TO THIS IN THE FIRST PLACE?
IT'S THE PRICE YOU HAVE TO PAY NOW THAT YOU'RE HAREWOOD'S FIRST FAMOUS RACING DRIVER.
AND NOW, IT IS MY GREAT PLEASURE TO INTRODUCE MY BROTHER, THE FASTEST DRIVER IN HAREWOOD, MARCH HARE!
THAT'S YOUR CUE! GO GO GO!

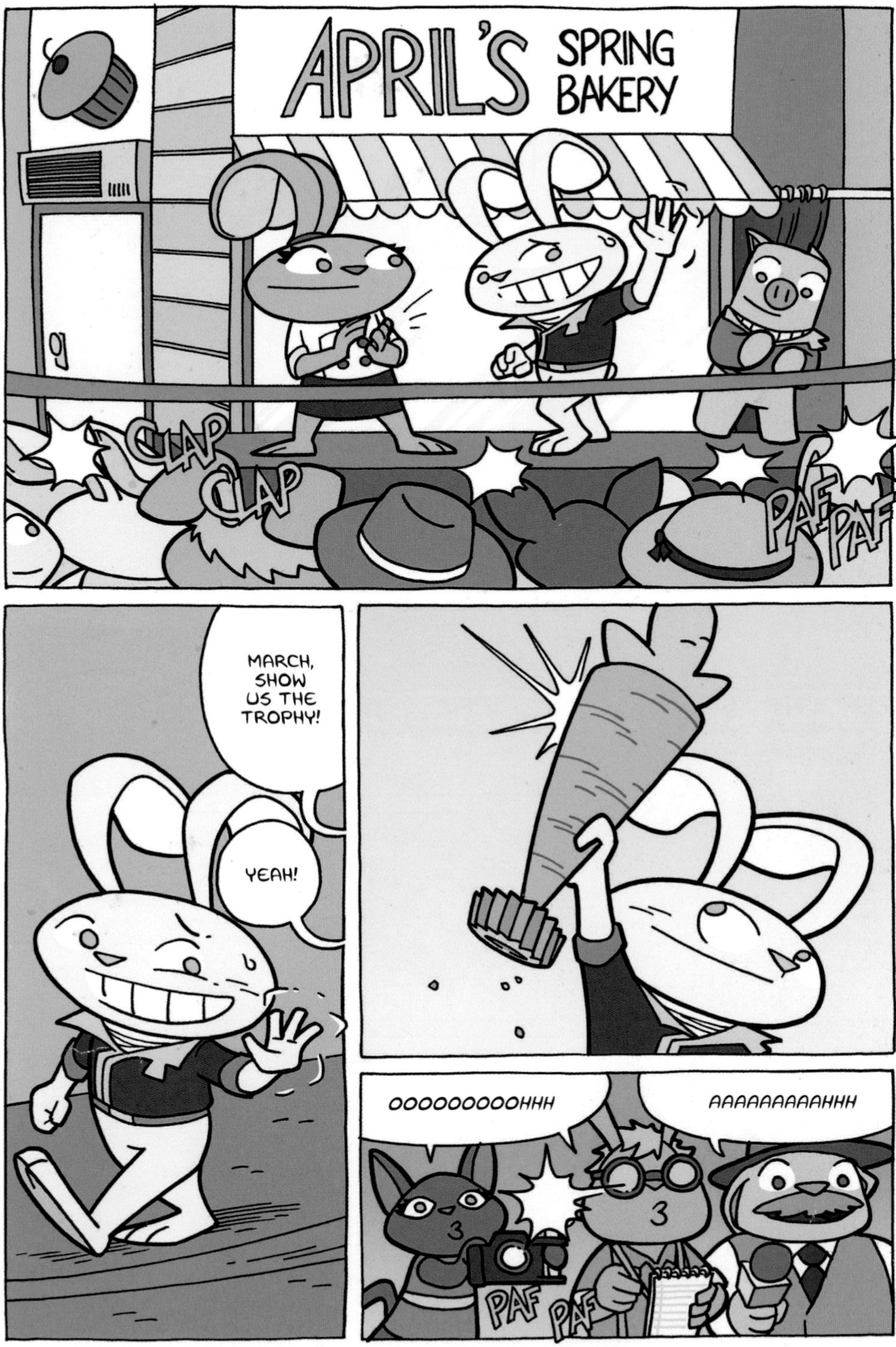
APRIL'S SPRING BAKERY
CLAP
CLAP
PAF
PAF
MARCH, SHOW US THE TROPHY!
YEAH!
OOOOOOOOOHHH
AAAAAAAAAHHH
PAF
PAF

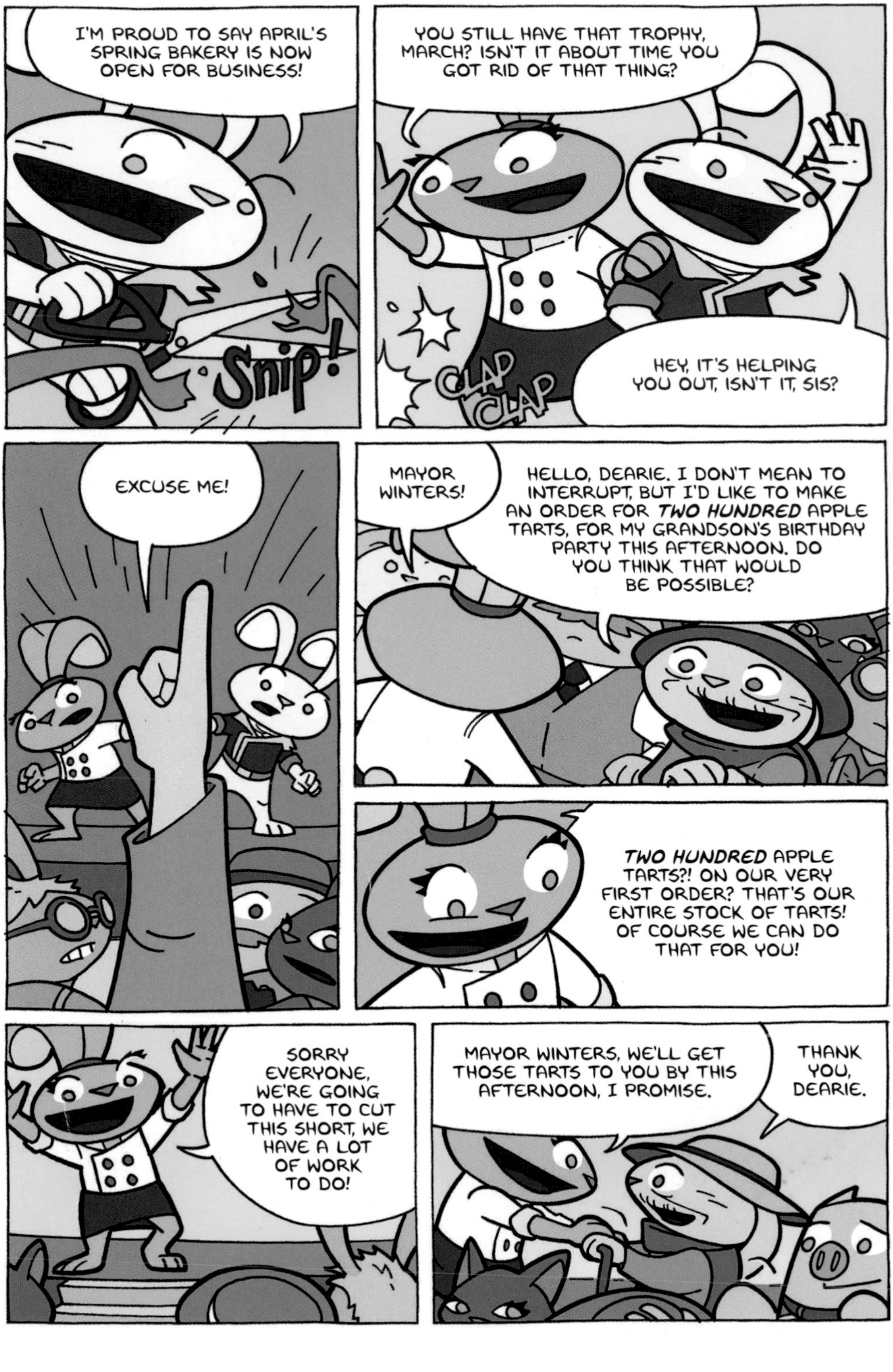
I'M PROUD TO SAY APRIL'S SPRING BAKERY IS NOW OPEN FOR BUSINESS!
SNIP!
YOU STILL HAVE THAT TROPHY, MARCH? ISN'T IT ABOUT TIME YOU GOT RID OF THAT THING?
CLAP CLAP
HEY, IT'S HELPING YOU OUT, ISN'T IT, SIS?
EXCUSE ME!
MAYOR WINTERS!
HELLO, DEARIE. I DON'T MEAN TO INTERRUPT, BUT I'D LIKE TO MAKE AN ORDER FOR *TWO HUNDRED* APPLE TARTS, FOR MY GRANDSON'S BIRTHDAY PARTY THIS AFTERNOON. DO YOU THINK THAT WOULD BE POSSIBLE?
TWO HUNDRED APPLE TARTS?! ON OUR VERY FIRST ORDER? THAT'S OUR ENTIRE STOCK OF TARTS! OF COURSE WE CAN DO THAT FOR YOU!
SORRY EVERYONE, WE'RE GOING TO HAVE TO CUT THIS SHORT, WE HAVE A LOT OF WORK TO DO!
MAYOR WINTERS, WE'LL GET THOSE TARTS TO YOU BY THIS AFTERNOON, I PROMISE.
THANK YOU, DEARIE.

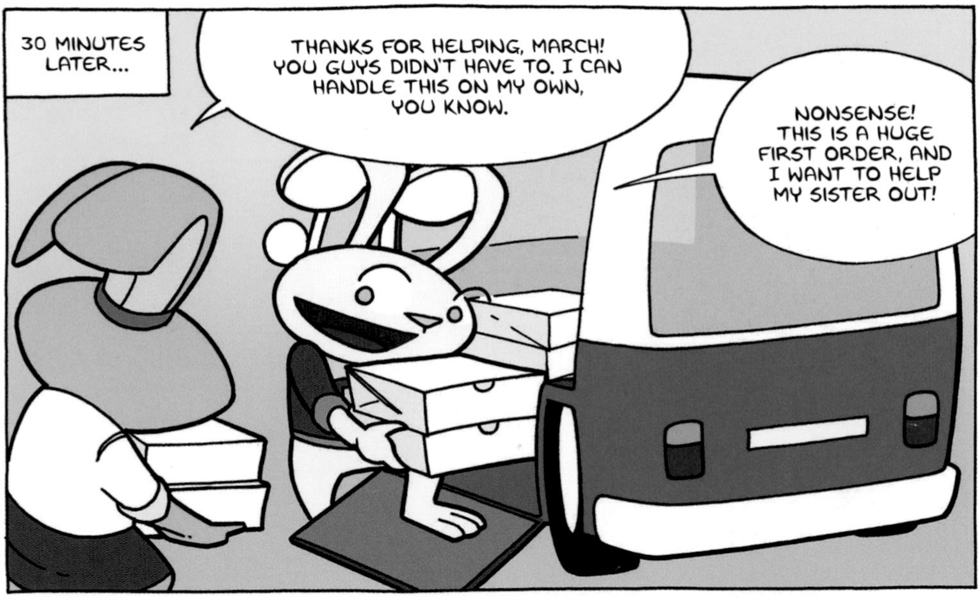
30 MINUTES LATER...
THANKS FOR HELPING, MARCH! YOU GUYS DIDN'T HAVE TO. I CAN HANDLE THIS ON MY OWN, YOU KNOW.
NONSENSE! THIS IS A HUGE FIRST ORDER, AND I WANT TO HELP MY SISTER OUT!

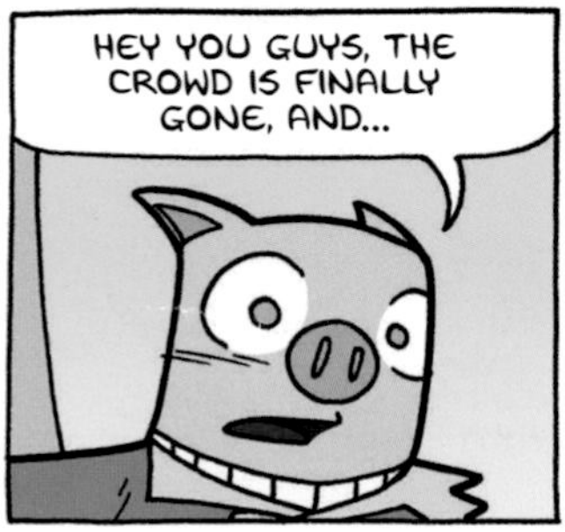
HEY YOU GUYS, THE CROWD IS FINALLY GONE, AND...

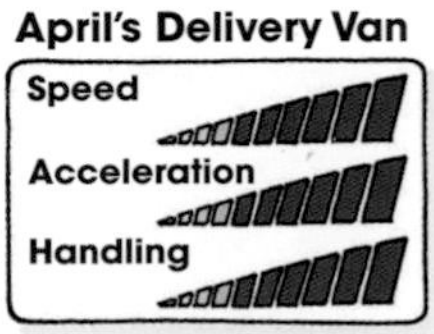
April's Delivery Van
Speed
Acceleration
Handling

Class: Cargo van
Layout: FF layout (Front-engine, Front-wheel-drive)

Engine: 2.2-Liter, flat four-cylinder (engine conversion)
Power: 142 hp
Torque: 149 lb/ft @3600 rpm

Transmission: 4-speed manual

Curb weight: 2,204 lb

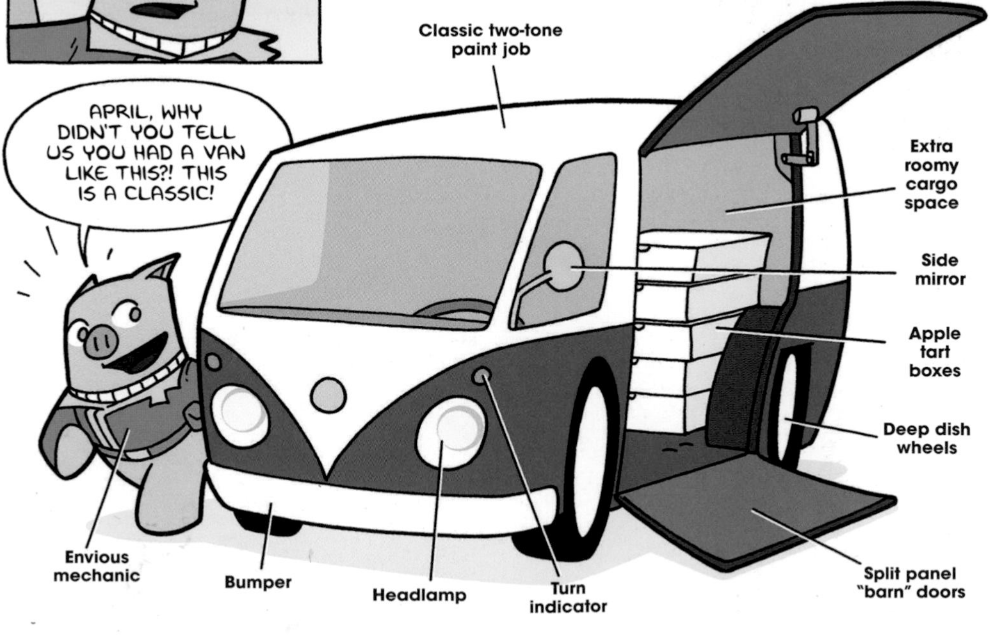
Classic two-tone paint job
APRIL, WHY DIDN'T YOU TELL US YOU HAD A VAN LIKE THIS?! THIS IS A CLASSIC!
Extra roomy cargo space
Side mirror
Apple tart boxes
Deep dish wheels
Envious mechanic
Bumper
Headlamp
Turn indicator
Split panel "barn" doors

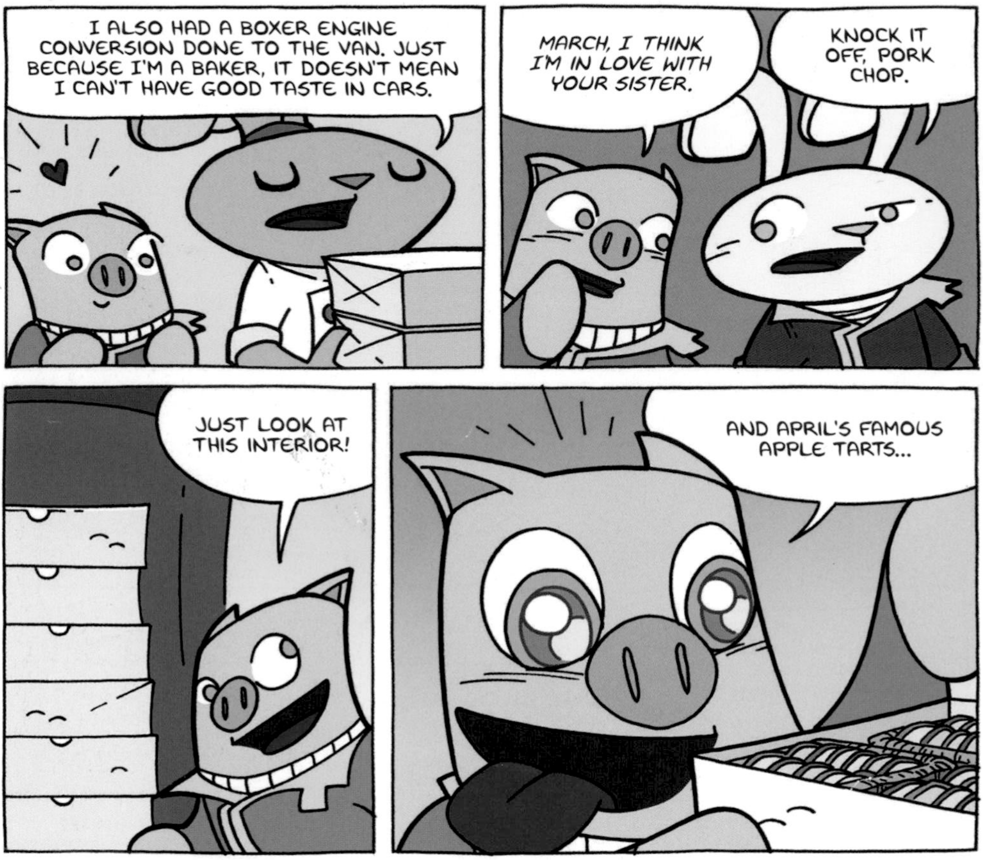
I ALSO HAD A BOXER ENGINE CONVERSION DONE TO THE VAN. JUST BECAUSE I'M A BAKER, IT DOESN'T MEAN I CAN'T HAVE GOOD TASTE IN CARS.
MARCH, I THINK I'M IN LOVE WITH YOUR SISTER.
KNOCK IT OFF, PORK CHOP.
JUST LOOK AT THIS INTERIOR!
AND APRIL'S FAMOUS APPLE TARTS...

April's Famous Apple Tart

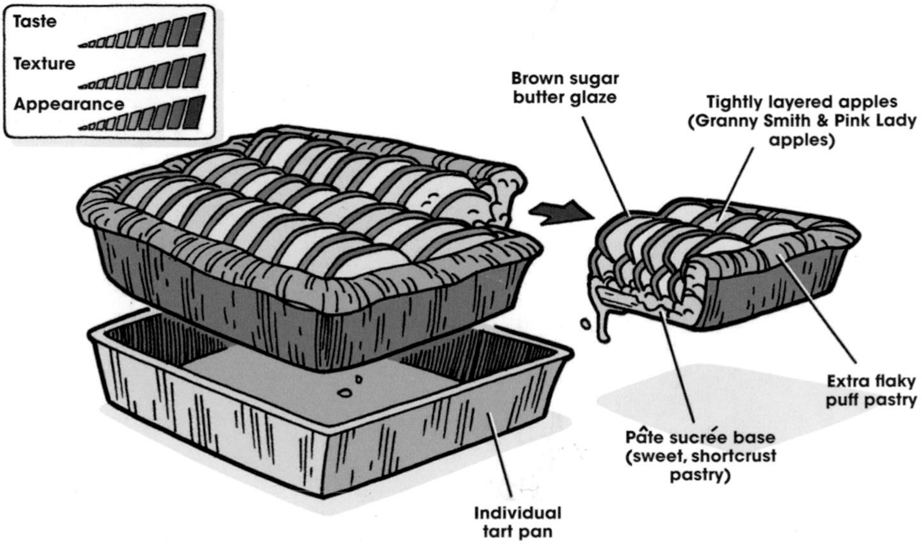
Taste
Texture
Appearance
Brown sugar butter glaze
Tightly layered apples (Granny Smith & Pink Lady apples)
Extra flaky puff pastry
Pâte sucrée base (sweet, shortcrust pastry)
Individual tart pan

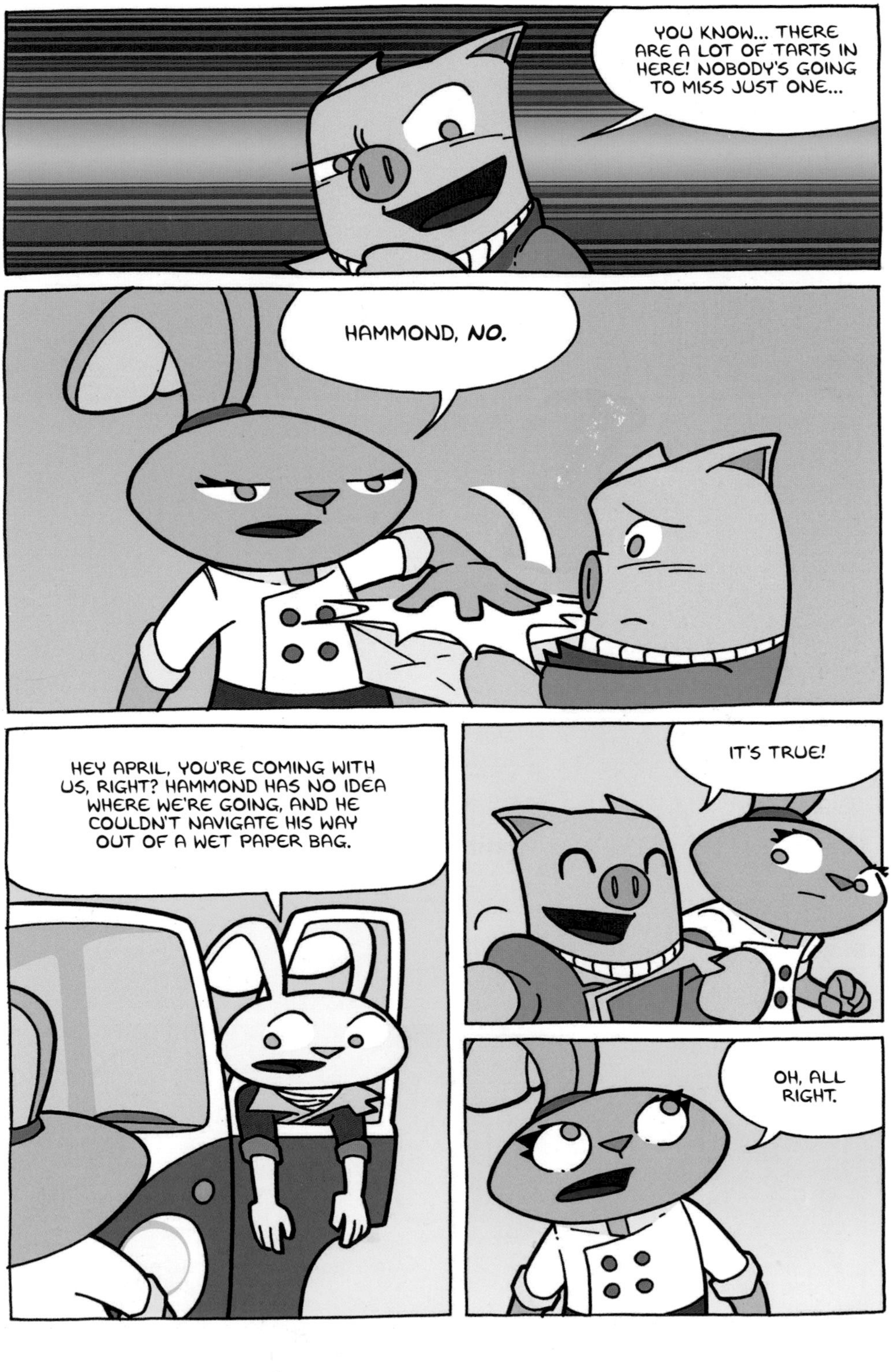
YOU KNOW... THERE ARE A LOT OF TARTS IN HERE! NOBODY'S GOING TO MISS JUST ONE...
HAMMOND, NO.
HEY APRIL, YOU'RE COMING WITH US, RIGHT? HAMMOND HAS NO IDEA WHERE WE'RE GOING, AND HE COULDN'T NAVIGATE HIS WAY OUT OF A WET PAPER BAG.
IT'S TRUE!
OH, ALL RIGHT.

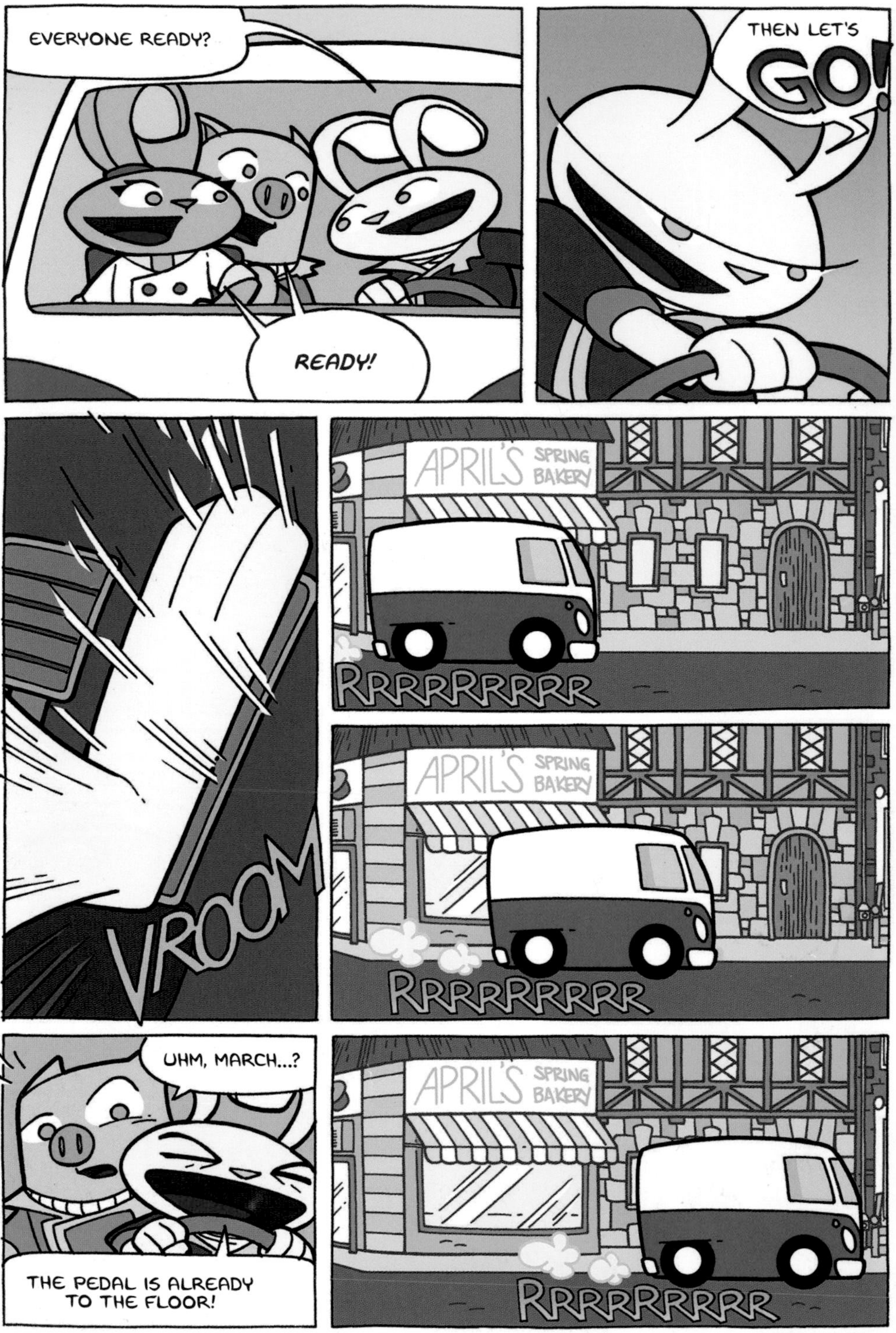
EVERYONE READY?
READY!
THEN LET'S
GO!
VROOM
APRIL'S SPRING BAKERY
RRRRRRRRR
APRIL'S SPRING BAKERY
RRRRRRRRR
UHM, MARCH...?
THE PEDAL IS ALREADY TO THE FLOOR!
APRIL'S SPRING BAKERY
RRRRRRRRR

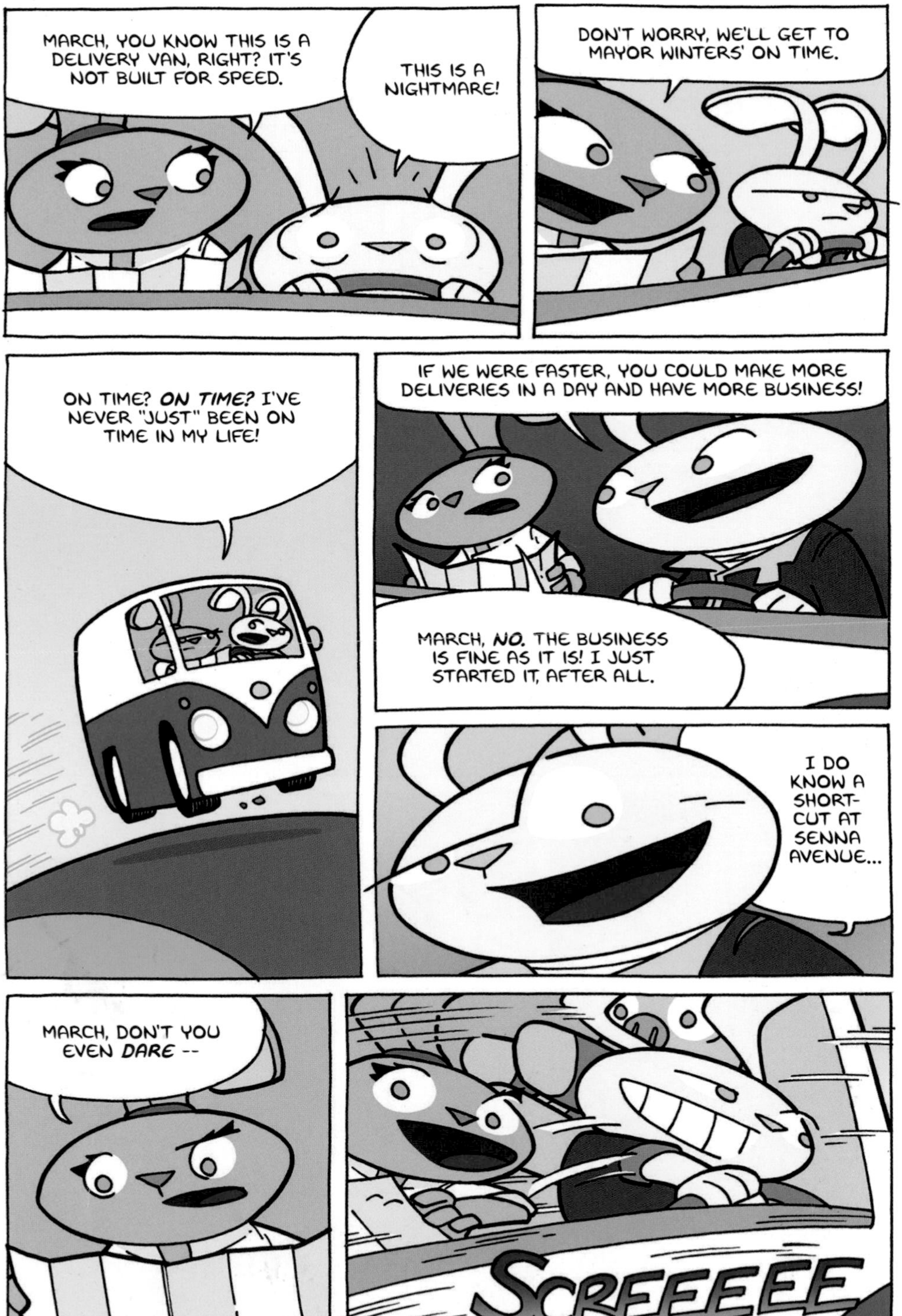
MARCH, YOU KNOW THIS IS A DELIVERY VAN, RIGHT? IT'S NOT BUILT FOR SPEED.
THIS IS A NIGHTMARE!
DON'T WORRY, WE'LL GET TO MAYOR WINTERS' ON TIME.
ON TIME? *ON TIME?* I'VE NEVER "JUST" BEEN ON TIME IN MY LIFE!
IF WE WERE FASTER, YOU COULD MAKE MORE DELIVERIES IN A DAY AND HAVE MORE BUSINESS!
MARCH, *NO.* THE BUSINESS IS FINE AS IT IS! I JUST STARTED IT, AFTER ALL.
I DO KNOW A SHORT-CUT AT SENNA AVENUE...
MARCH, DON'T YOU EVEN *DARE* --
SCREEEEE

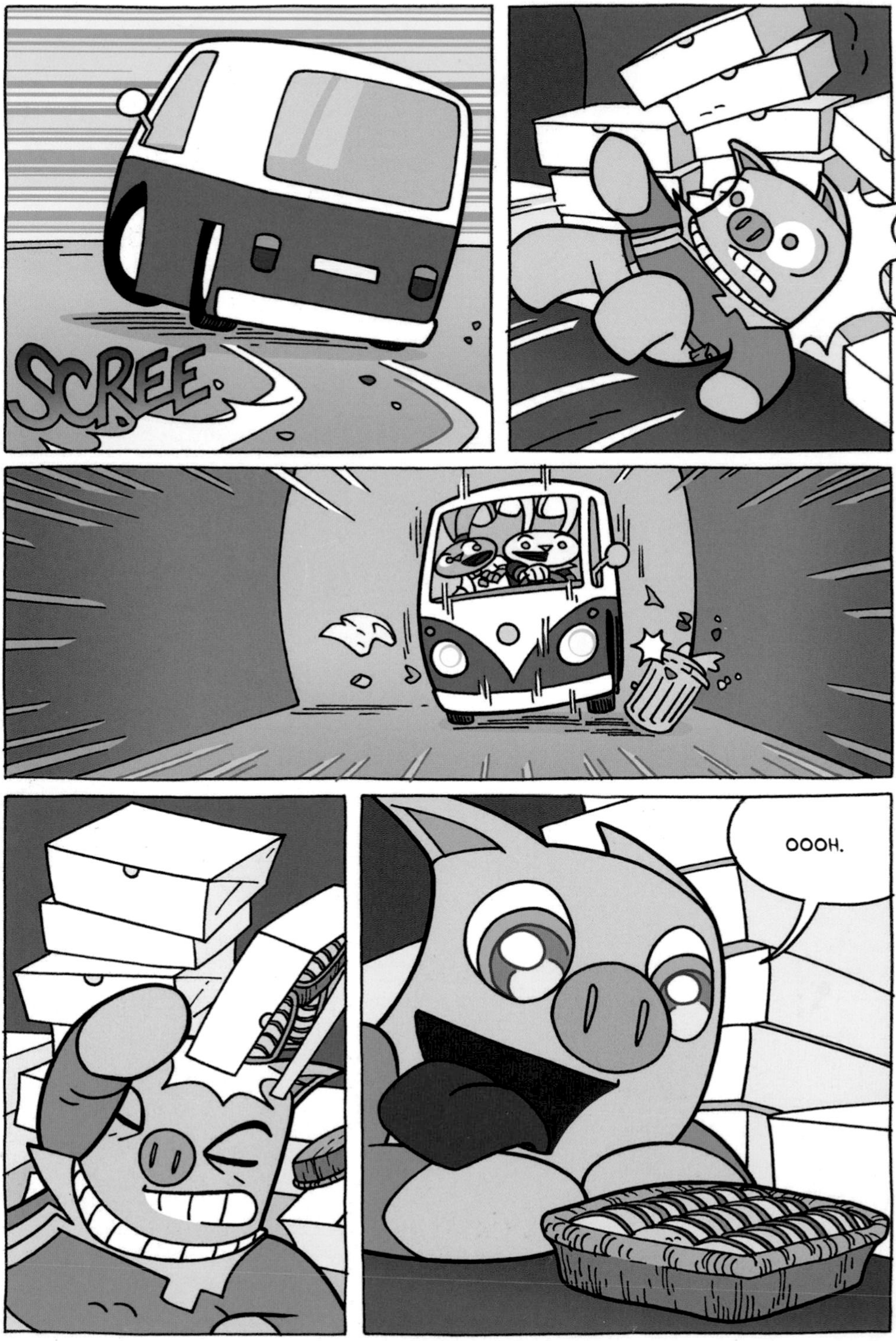
SCREE
OOOH.

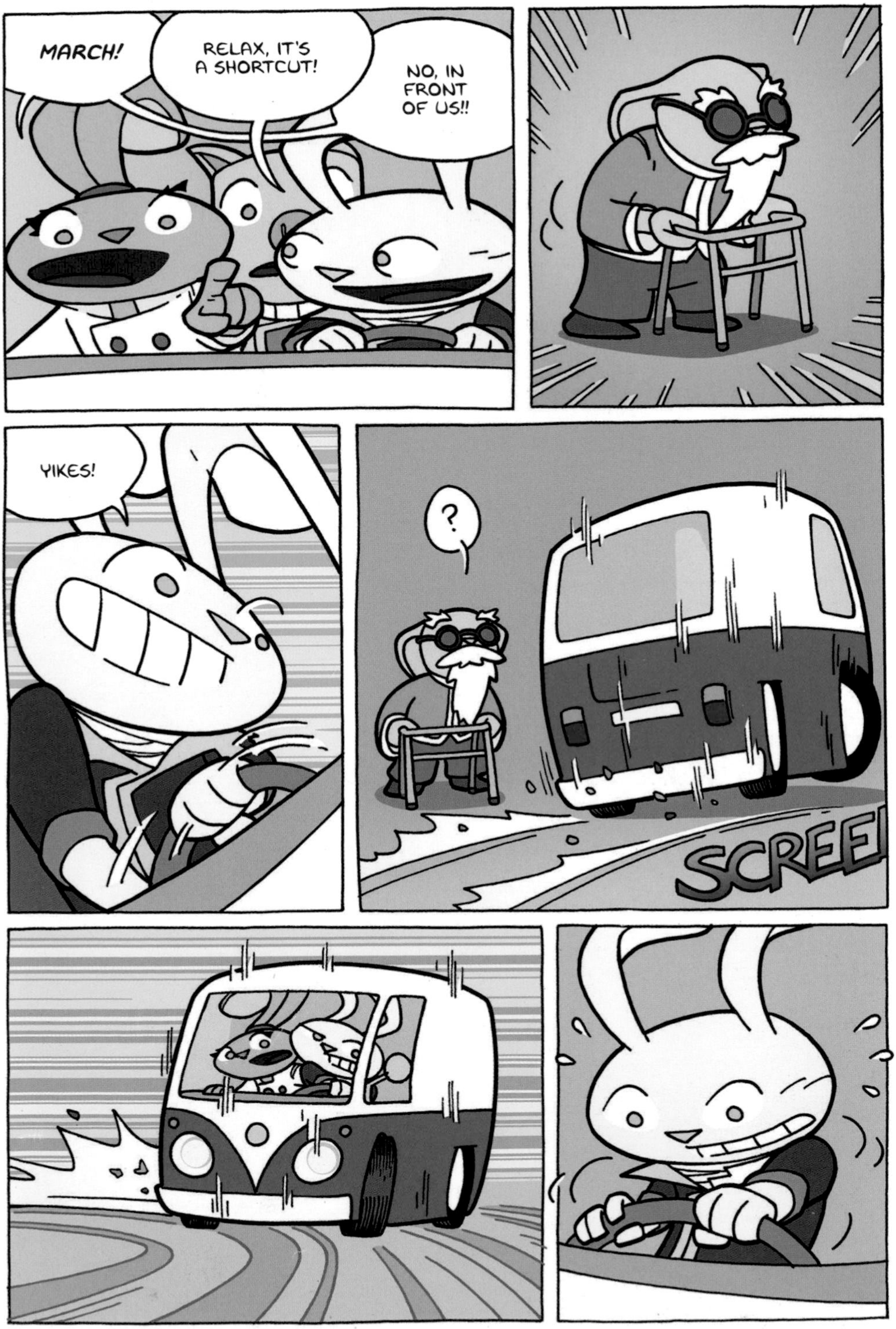
MARCH!
RELAX, IT'S A SHORTCUT!
NO, IN FRONT OF US!!
YIKES!
?
SCREE

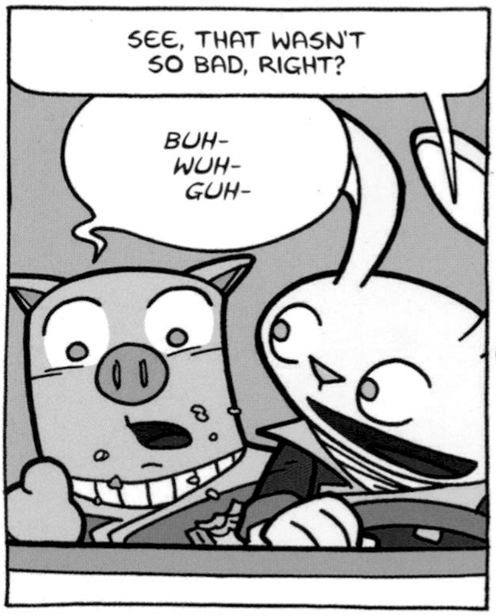
SEE, THAT WASN'T SO BAD, RIGHT?
BUH- WUH- GUH-

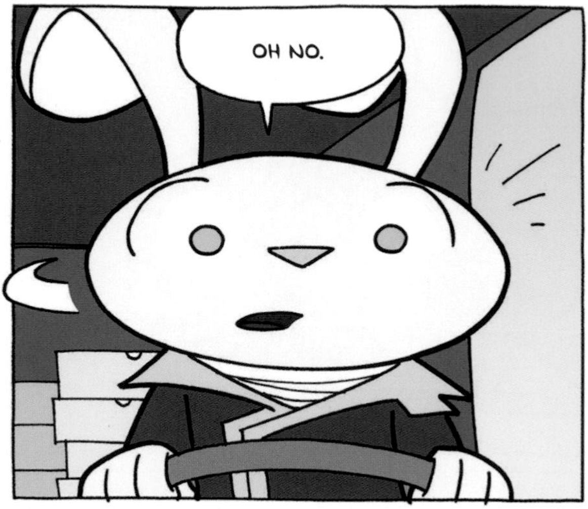
OH NO.

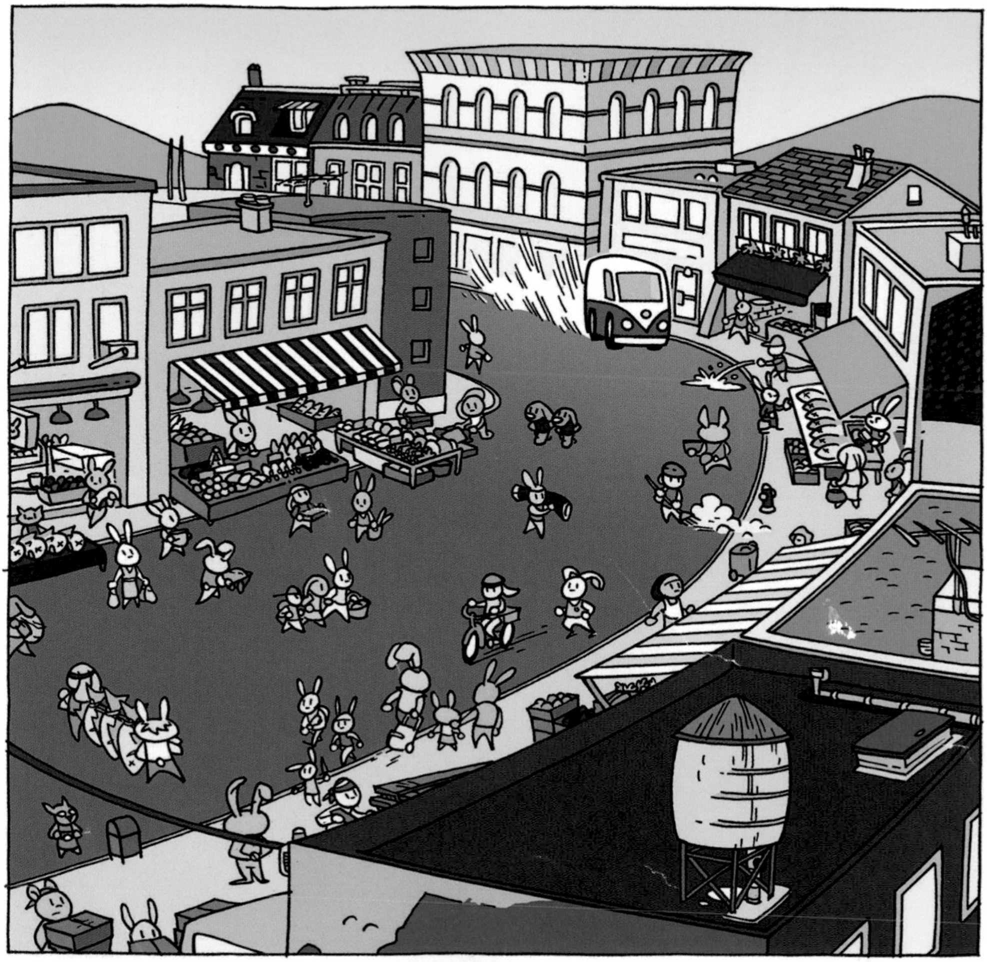

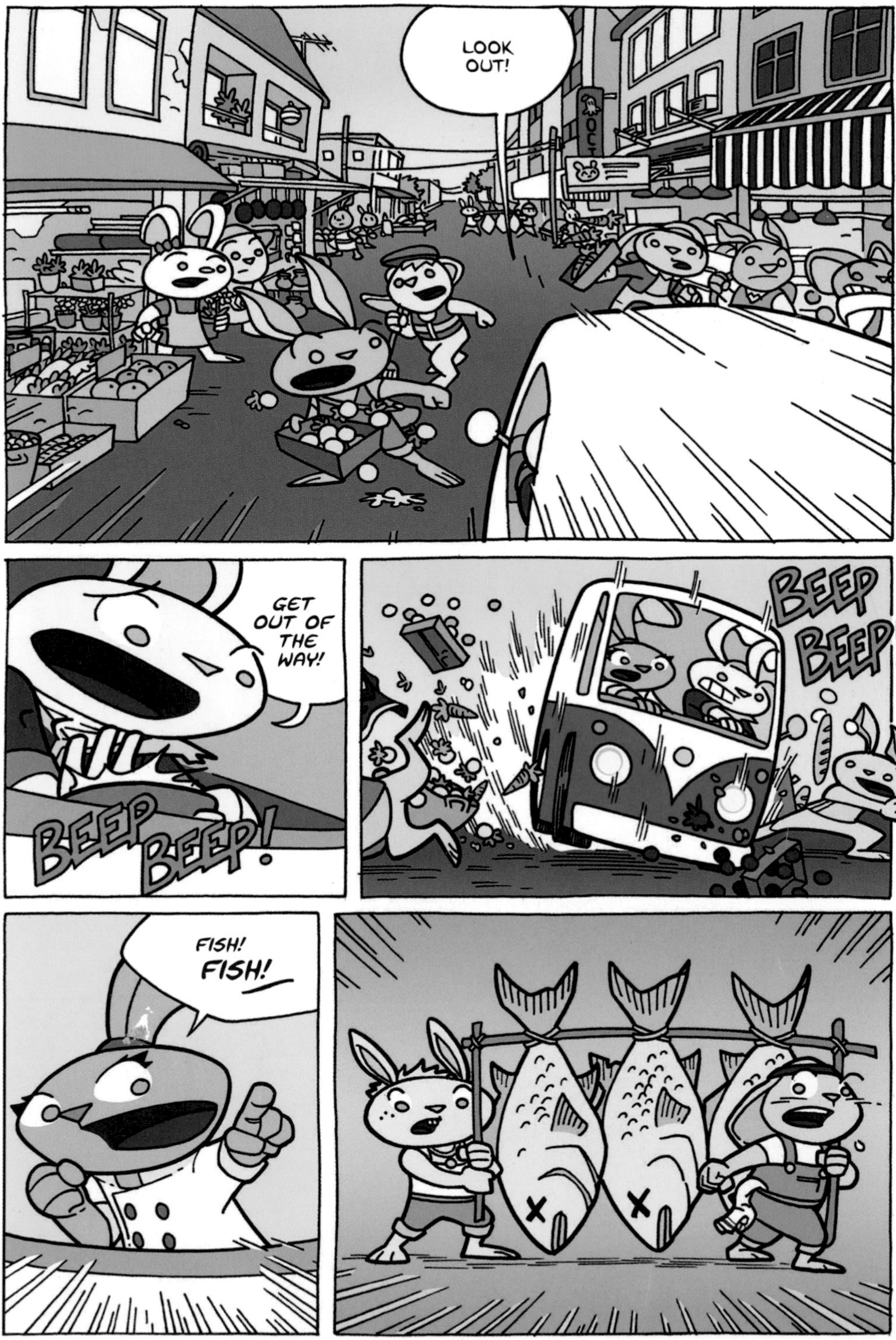
LOOK OUT!
GET OUT OF THE WAY!
BEEP BEEP!
BEEP BEEP!
FISH! FISH!

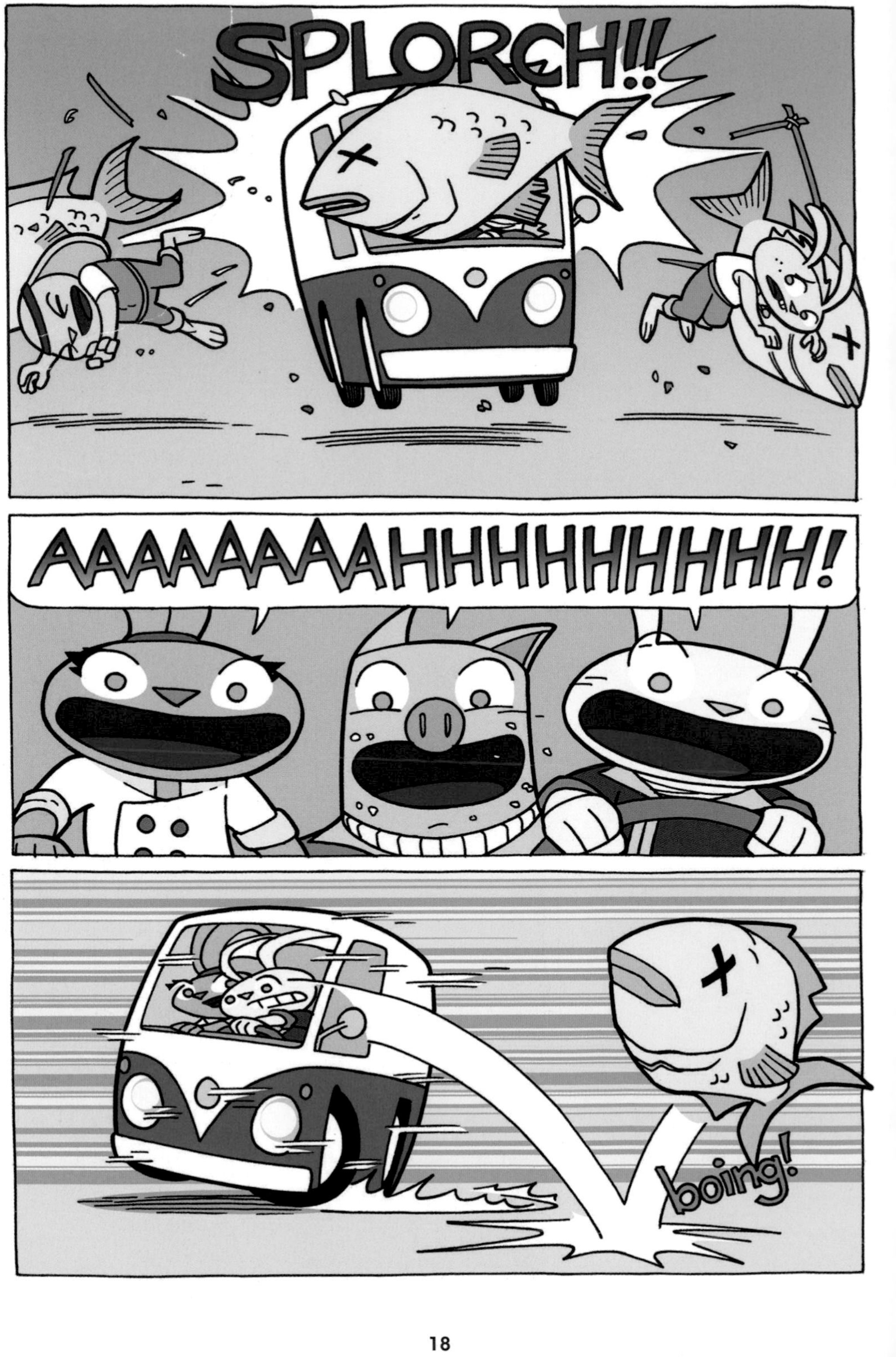
SPLORCH!!
AAAAAAAAHHHHHHHHHH!
boing!

HOLD ON!

KRUNCH!

AAAAH

AAAAAAAAAHHHHHHH

19

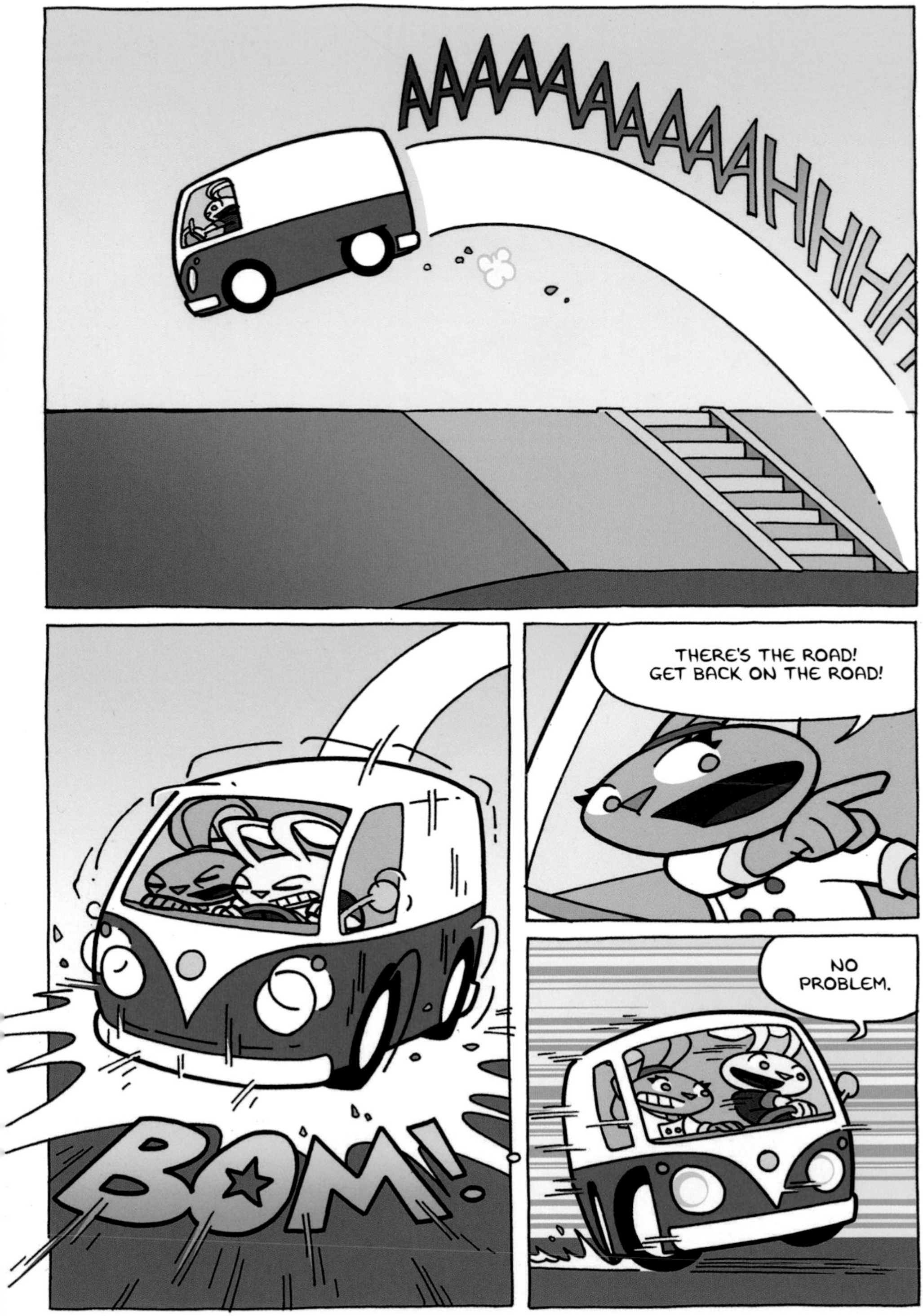
AAAAAAAAAAAHHHHH
BOM!
THERE'S THE ROAD! GET BACK ON THE ROAD!
NO PROBLEM.

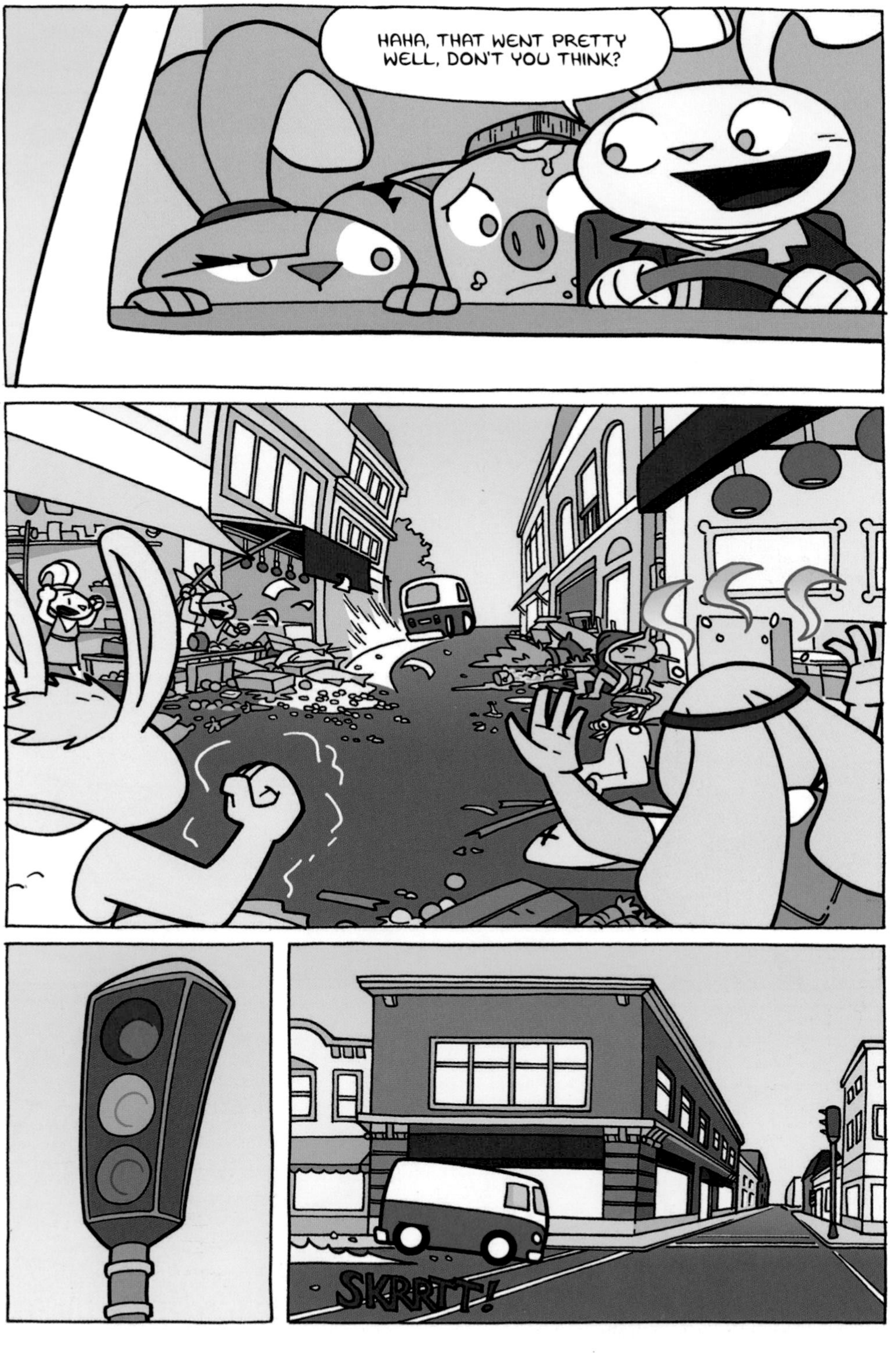
HAHA, THAT WENT PRETTY WELL, DON'T YOU THINK?
SKRRTT!

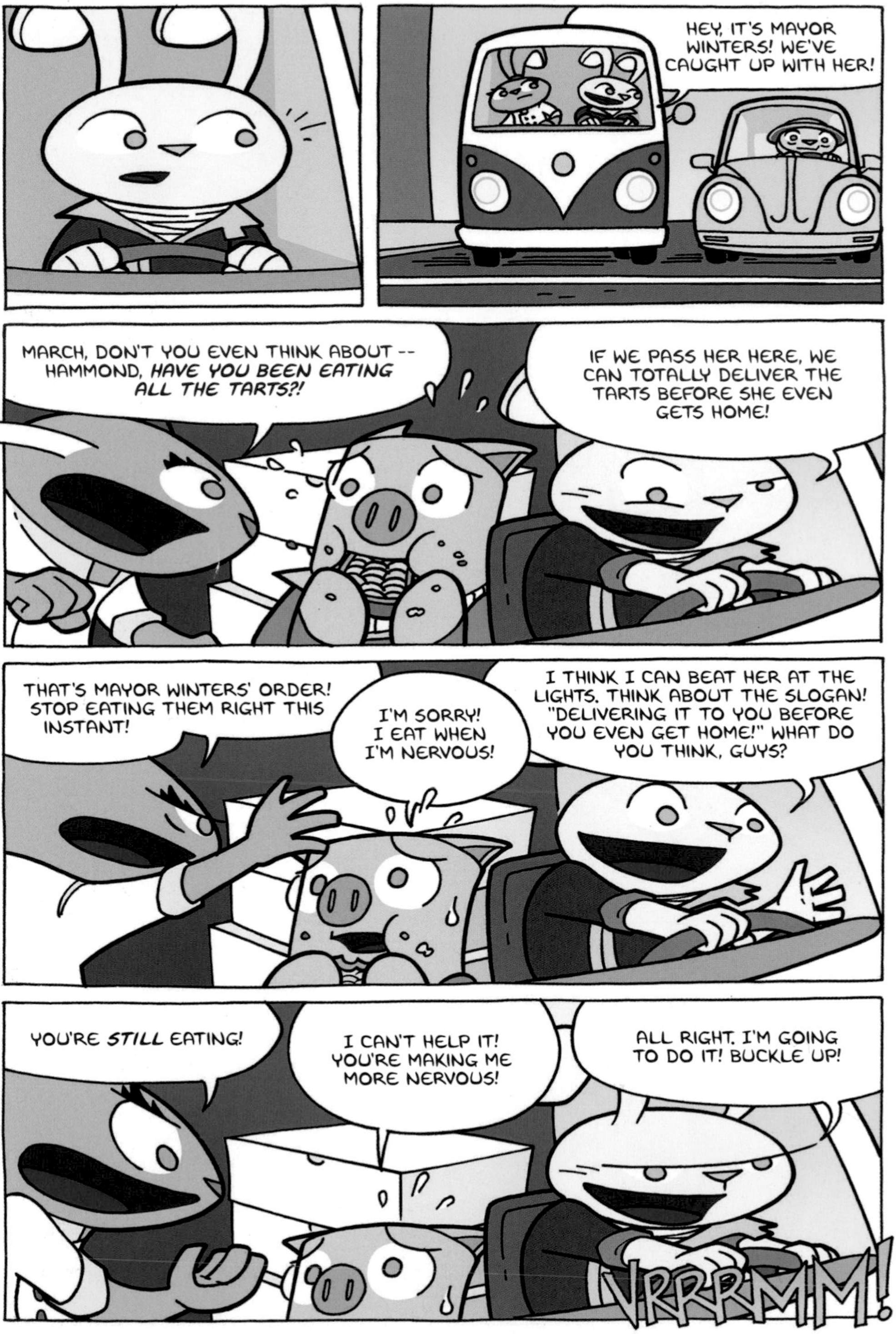
HEY, IT'S MAYOR WINTERS! WE'VE CAUGHT UP WITH HER!
MARCH, DON'T YOU EVEN THINK ABOUT -- HAMMOND, *HAVE YOU BEEN EATING ALL THE TARTS?!*
IF WE PASS HER HERE, WE CAN TOTALLY DELIVER THE TARTS BEFORE SHE EVEN GETS HOME!
THAT'S MAYOR WINTERS' ORDER! STOP EATING THEM RIGHT THIS INSTANT!
I'M SORRY! I EAT WHEN I'M NERVOUS!
I THINK I CAN BEAT HER AT THE LIGHTS. THINK ABOUT THE SLOGAN! "DELIVERING IT TO YOU BEFORE YOU EVEN GET HOME!" WHAT DO YOU THINK, GUYS?
YOU'RE *STILL* EATING!
I CAN'T HELP IT! YOU'RE MAKING ME MORE NERVOUS!
ALL RIGHT. I'M GOING TO DO IT! BUCKLE UP!
VRRRMMM!

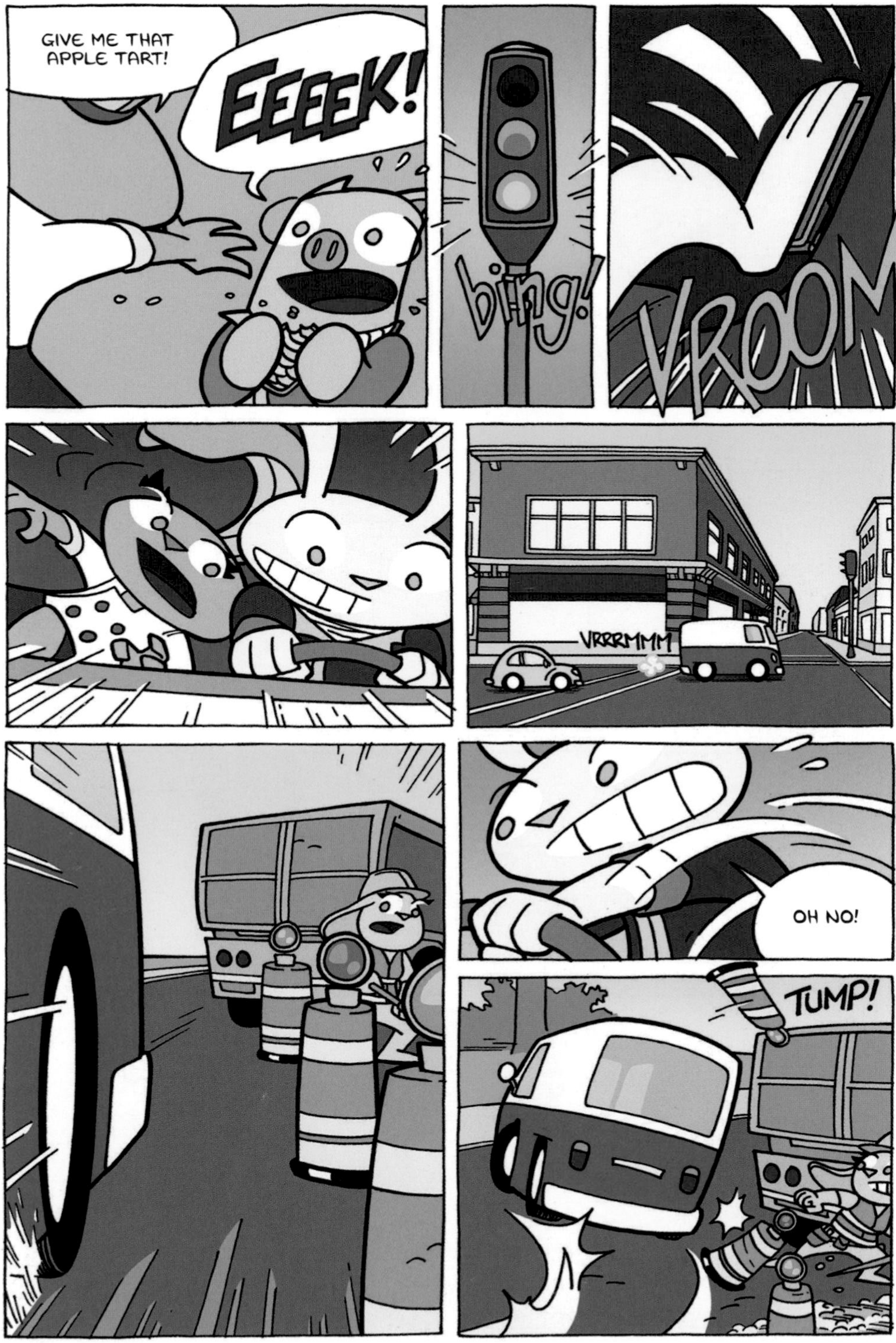
GIVE ME THAT APPLE TART!
EEEEK!
bing!
VROOM
VRRRMMM
OH NO!
TUMP!

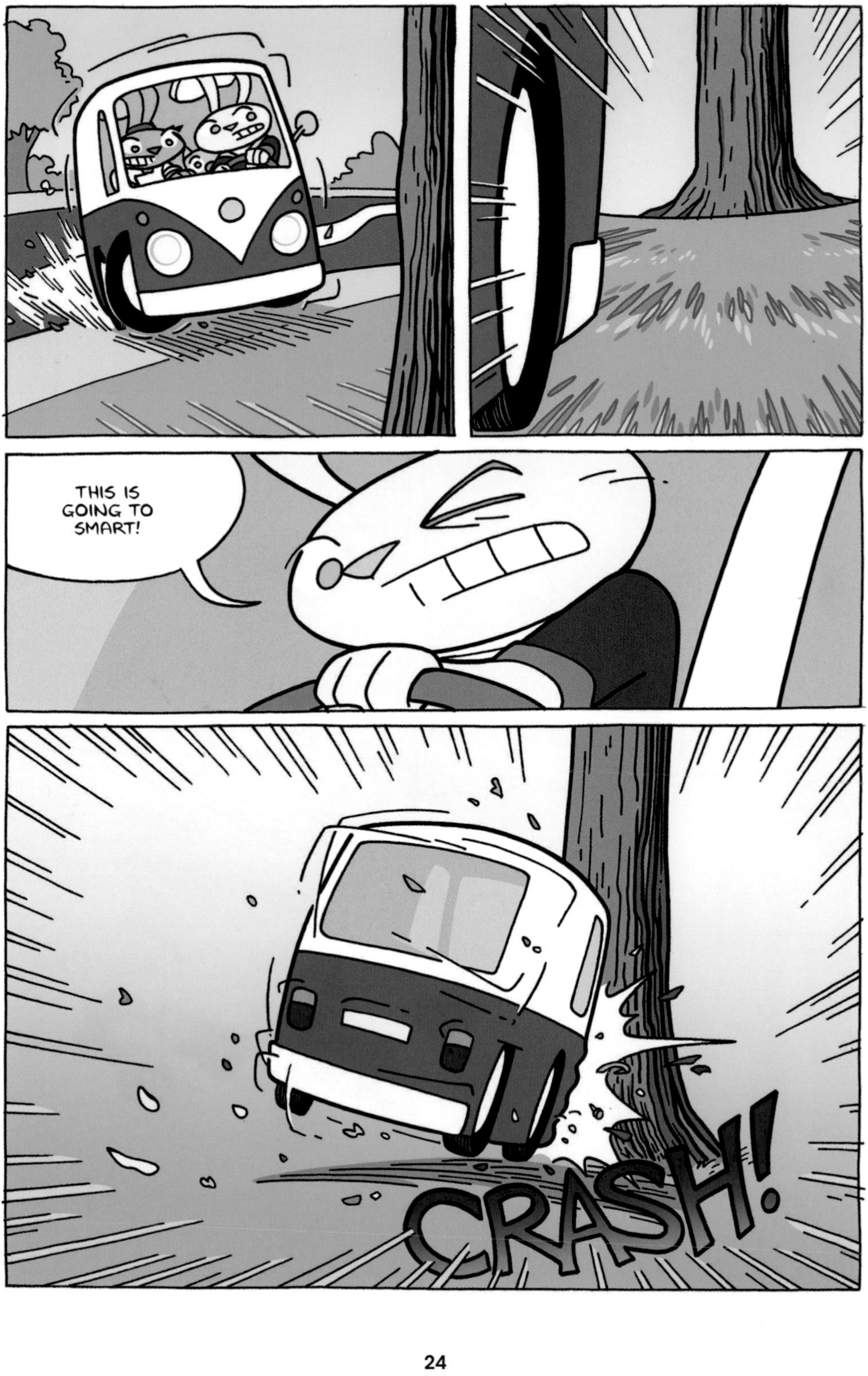
THIS IS GOING TO SMART!
CRASH!

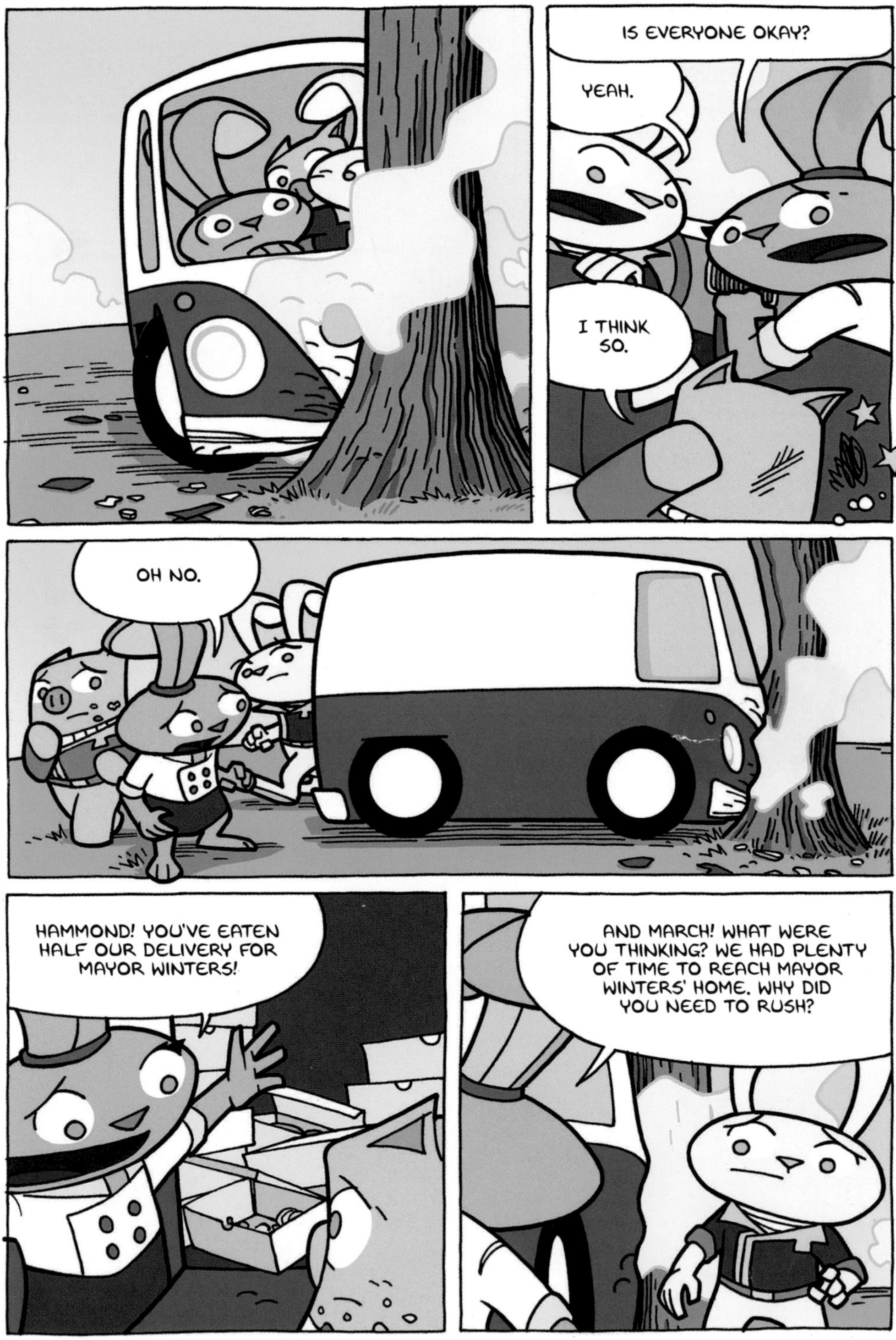
IS EVERYONE OKAY?
YEAH.
I THINK SO.
OH NO.
HAMMOND! YOU'VE EATEN HALF OUR DELIVERY FOR MAYOR WINTERS!
AND MARCH! WHAT WERE YOU THINKING? WE HAD PLENTY OF TIME TO REACH MAYOR WINTERS' HOME. WHY DID YOU NEED TO RUSH?

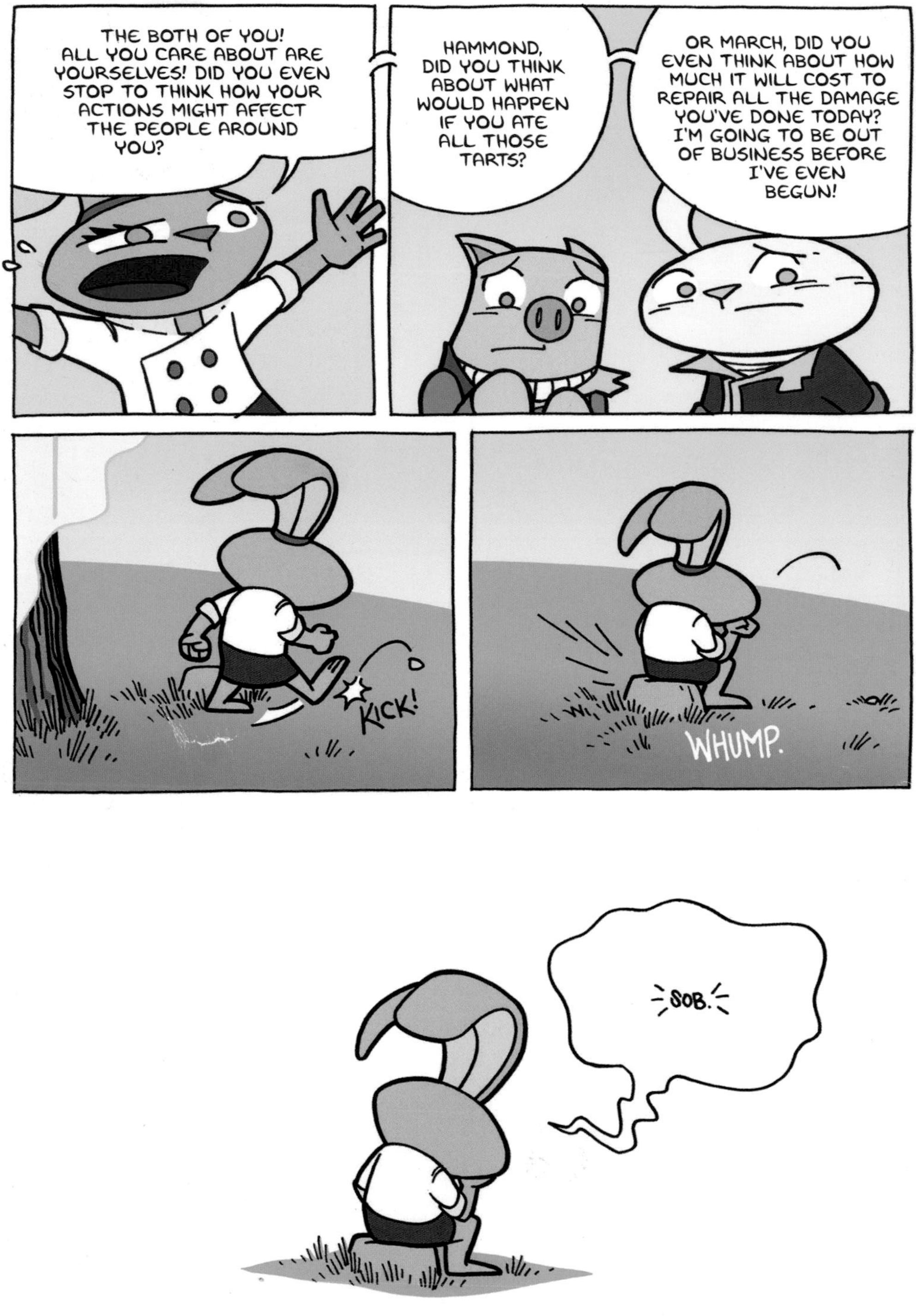
THE BOTH OF YOU! ALL YOU CARE ABOUT ARE YOURSELVES! DID YOU EVEN STOP TO THINK HOW YOUR ACTIONS MIGHT AFFECT THE PEOPLE AROUND YOU?
HAMMOND, DID YOU THINK ABOUT WHAT WOULD HAPPEN IF YOU ATE ALL THOSE TARTS?
OR MARCH, DID YOU EVEN THINK ABOUT HOW MUCH IT WILL COST TO REPAIR ALL THE DAMAGE YOU'VE DONE TODAY? I'M GOING TO BE OUT OF BUSINESS BEFORE I'VE EVEN BEGUN!
KICK!
WHUMP.
SOB.

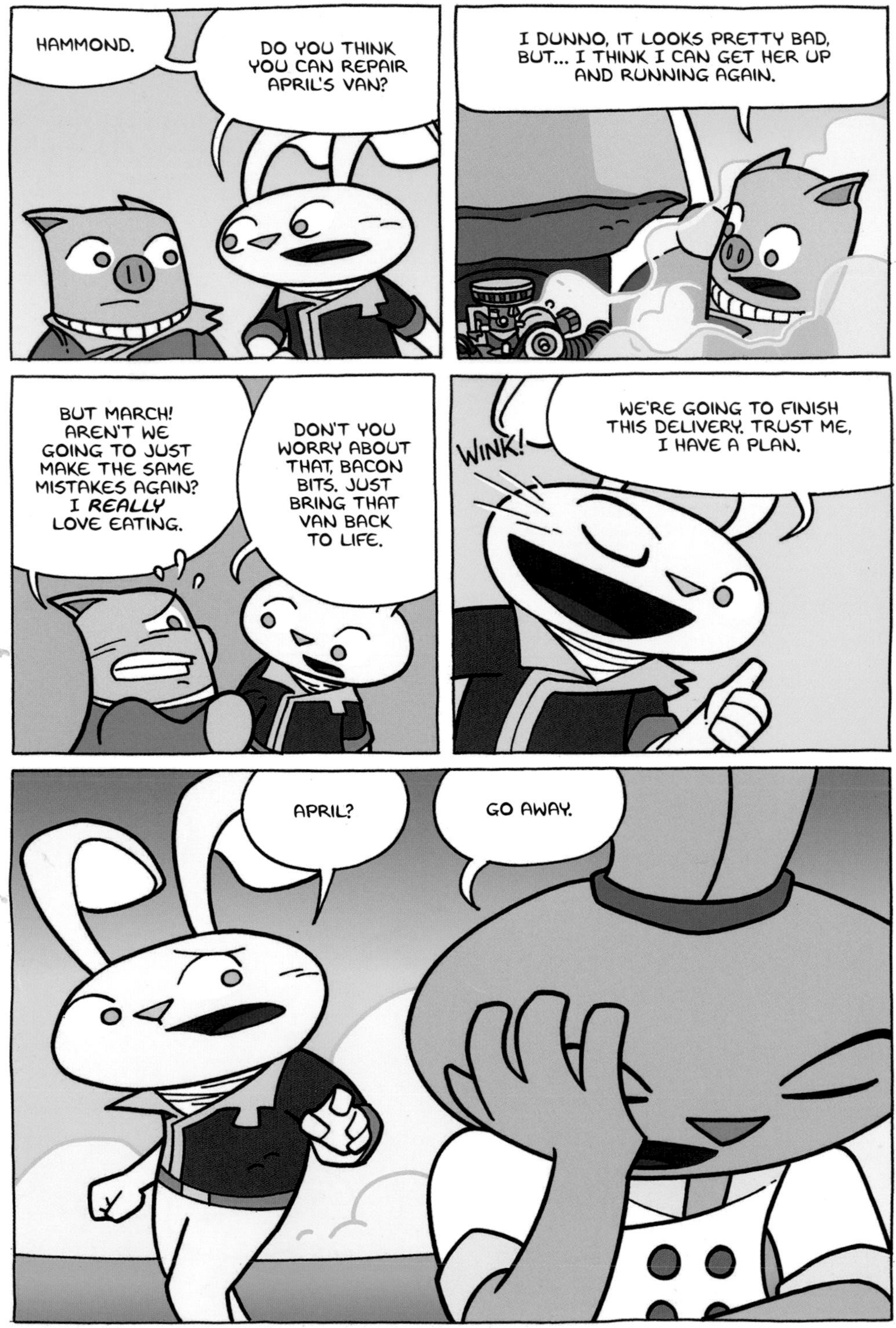
HAMMOND.
DO YOU THINK YOU CAN REPAIR APRIL'S VAN?
I DUNNO, IT LOOKS PRETTY BAD, BUT... I THINK I CAN GET HER UP AND RUNNING AGAIN.
BUT MARCH! AREN'T WE GOING TO JUST MAKE THE SAME MISTAKES AGAIN? I REALLY LOVE EATING.
DON'T YOU WORRY ABOUT THAT, BACON BITS. JUST BRING THAT VAN BACK TO LIFE.
WINK!
WE'RE GOING TO FINISH THIS DELIVERY. TRUST ME, I HAVE A PLAN.
APRIL?
GO AWAY.

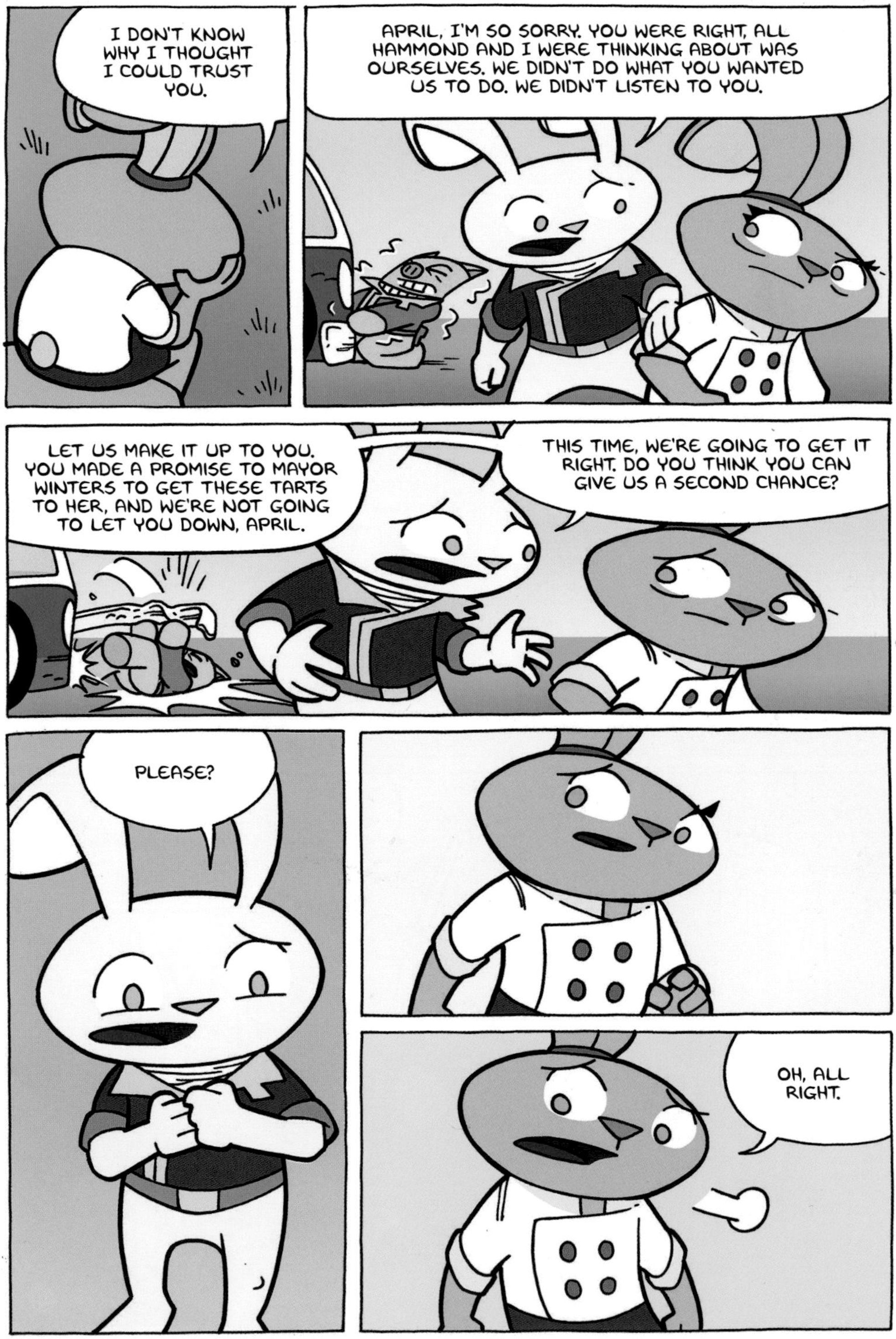
I DON'T KNOW WHY I THOUGHT I COULD TRUST YOU.
APRIL, I'M SO SORRY. YOU WERE RIGHT. ALL HAMMOND AND I WERE THINKING ABOUT WAS OURSELVES. WE DIDN'T DO WHAT YOU WANTED US TO DO. WE DIDN'T LISTEN TO YOU.
LET US MAKE IT UP TO YOU. YOU MADE A PROMISE TO MAYOR WINTERS TO GET THESE TARTS TO HER, AND WE'RE NOT GOING TO LET YOU DOWN, APRIL.
THIS TIME, WE'RE GOING TO GET IT RIGHT. DO YOU THINK YOU CAN GIVE US A SECOND CHANCE?
PLEASE?
OH, ALL RIGHT.

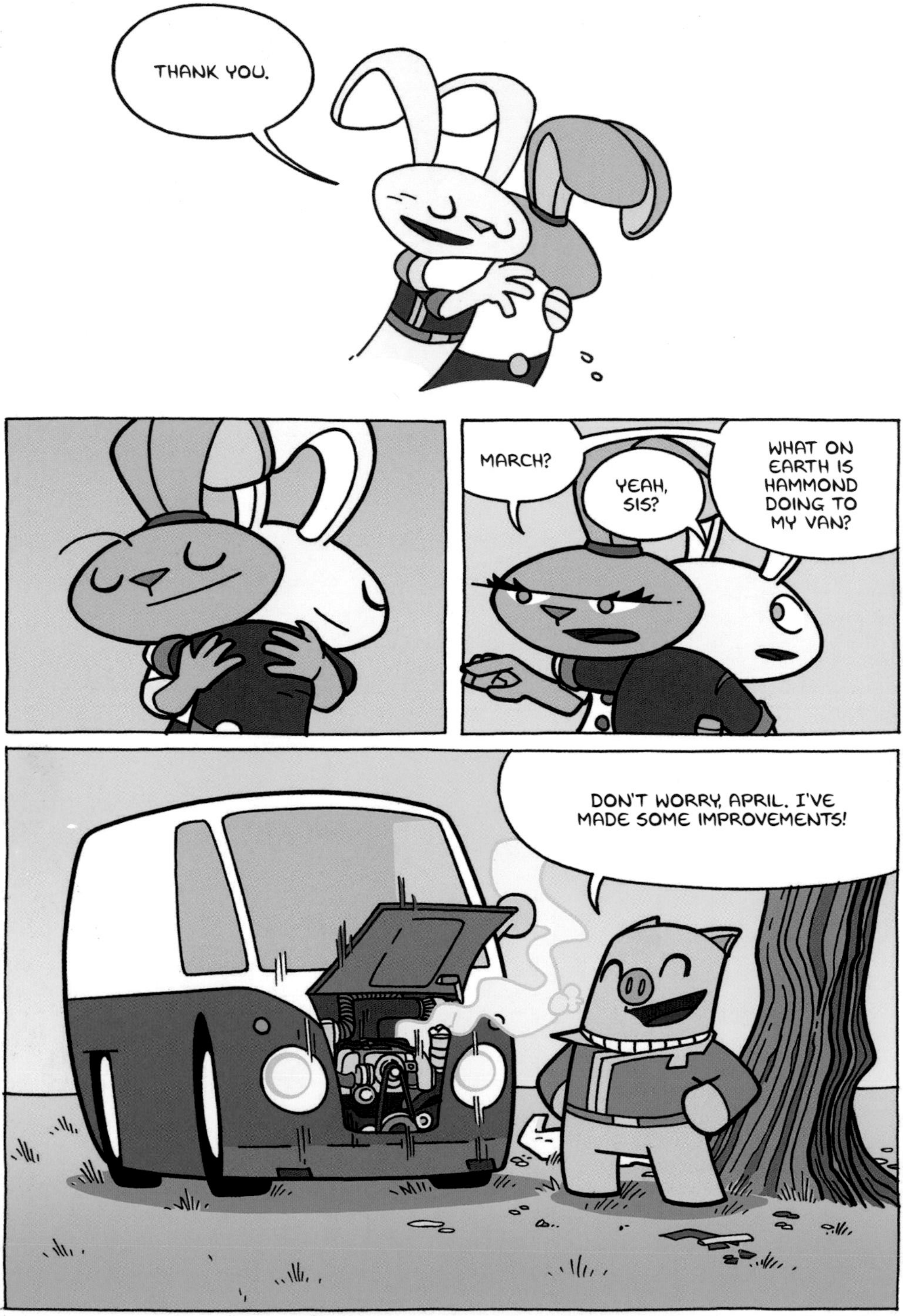
THANK YOU.
MARCH?
YEAH, SIS?
WHAT ON EARTH IS HAMMOND DOING TO MY VAN?
DON'T WORRY, APRIL. I'VE MADE SOME IMPROVEMENTS!

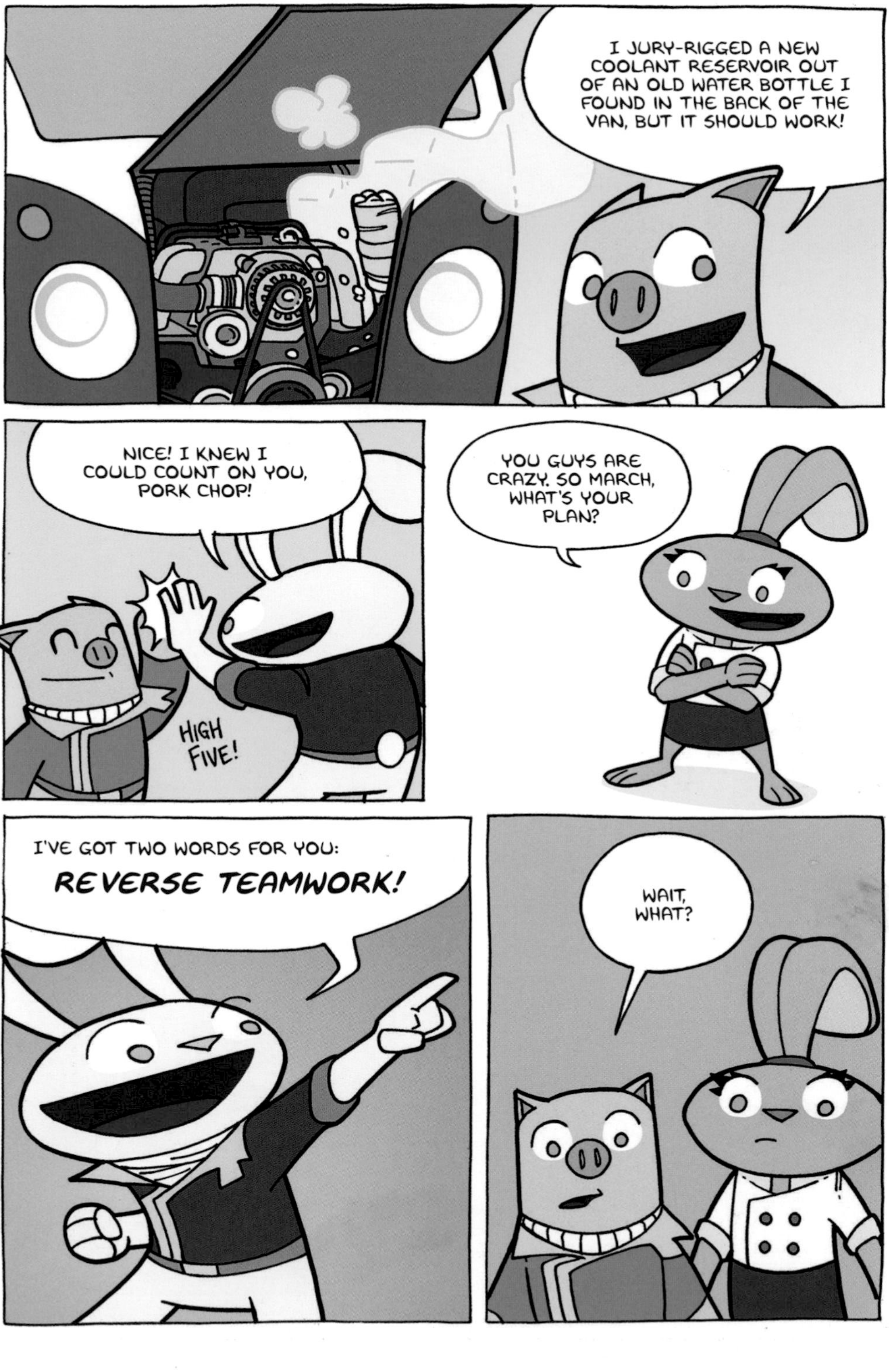
I JURY-RIGGED A NEW COOLANT RESERVOIR OUT OF AN OLD WATER BOTTLE I FOUND IN THE BACK OF THE VAN, BUT IT SHOULD WORK!
NICE! I KNEW I COULD COUNT ON YOU, PORK CHOP!
HIGH FIVE!
YOU GUYS ARE CRAZY. SO MARCH, WHAT'S YOUR PLAN?
I'VE GOT TWO WORDS FOR YOU:
REVERSE TEAMWORK!
WAIT, WHAT?

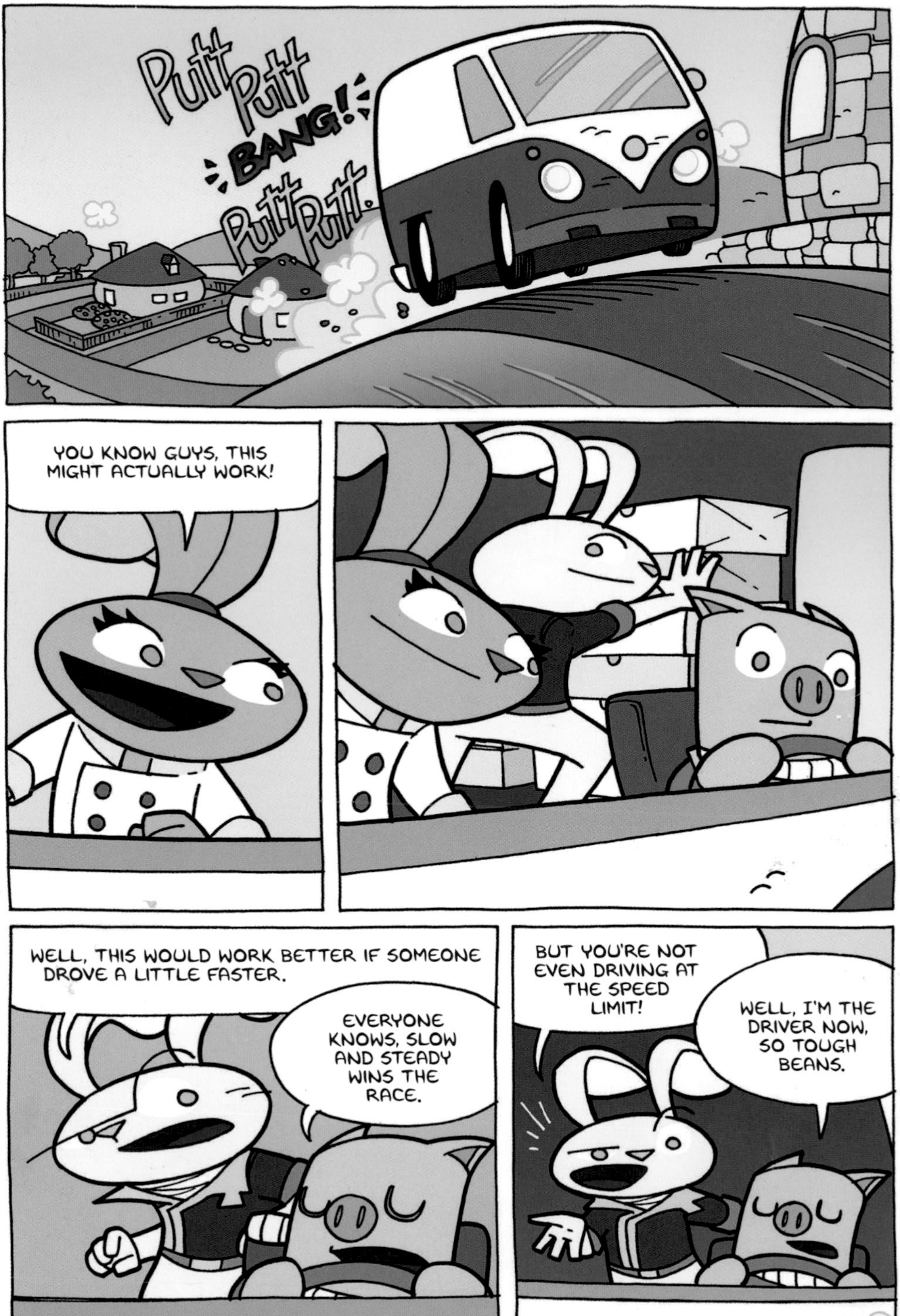
Putt Putt
BANG!
Putt Putt.
YOU KNOW GUYS, THIS MIGHT ACTUALLY WORK!
WELL, THIS WOULD WORK BETTER IF SOMEONE DROVE A LITTLE FASTER.
EVERYONE KNOWS, SLOW AND STEADY WINS THE RACE.
BUT YOU'RE NOT EVEN DRIVING AT THE SPEED LIMIT!
WELL, I'M THE DRIVER NOW, SO TOUGH BEANS.

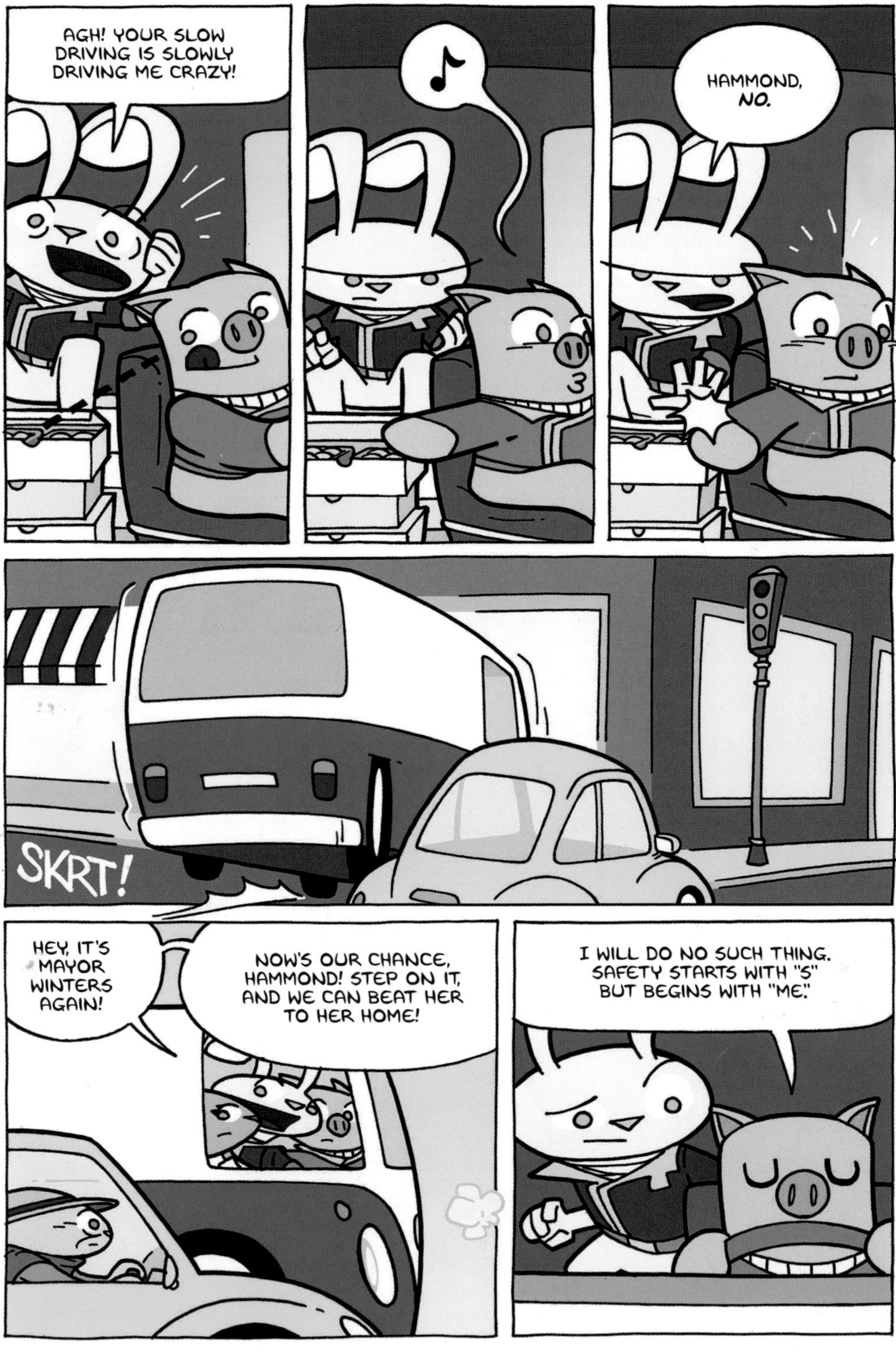
AGH! YOUR SLOW DRIVING IS SLOWLY DRIVING ME CRAZY!
♪
HAMMOND, NO.
SKRT!
HEY, IT'S MAYOR WINTERS AGAIN!
NOW'S OUR CHANCE, HAMMOND! STEP ON IT, AND WE CAN BEAT HER TO HER HOME!
I WILL DO NO SUCH THING. SAFETY STARTS WITH "S" BUT BEGINS WITH "ME."

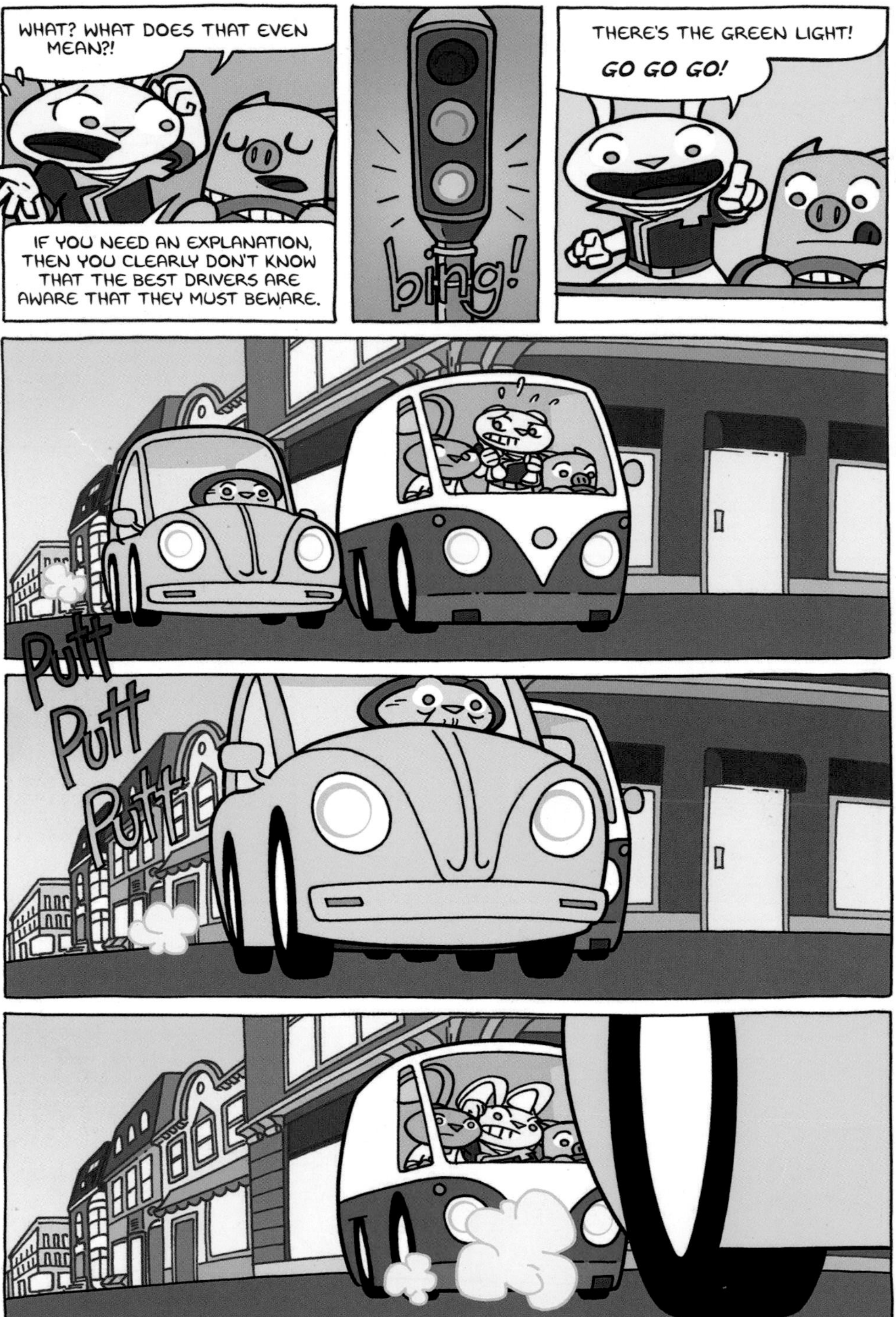
WHAT? WHAT DOES THAT EVEN MEAN?!
IF YOU NEED AN EXPLANATION, THEN YOU CLEARLY DON'T KNOW THAT THE BEST DRIVERS ARE AWARE THAT THEY MUST BEWARE.
bing!
THERE'S THE GREEN LIGHT!
GO GO GO!
Putt
Putt
Putt

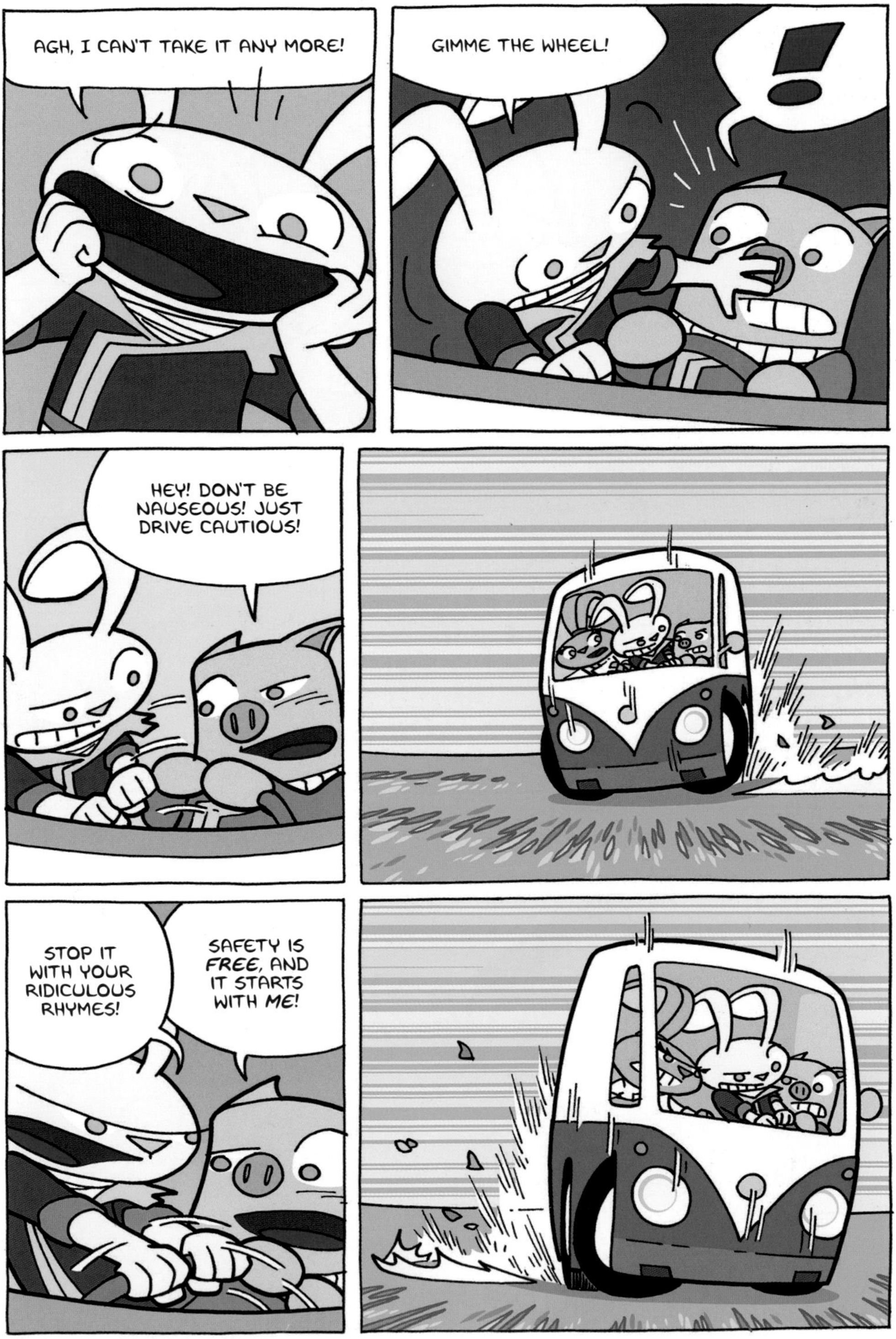
AGH, I CAN'T TAKE IT ANY MORE!
GIMME THE WHEEL!
!
HEY! DON'T BE NAUSEOUS! JUST DRIVE CAUTIOUS!
STOP IT WITH YOUR RIDICULOUS RHYMES!
SAFETY IS *FREE*, AND IT STARTS WITH *ME*!

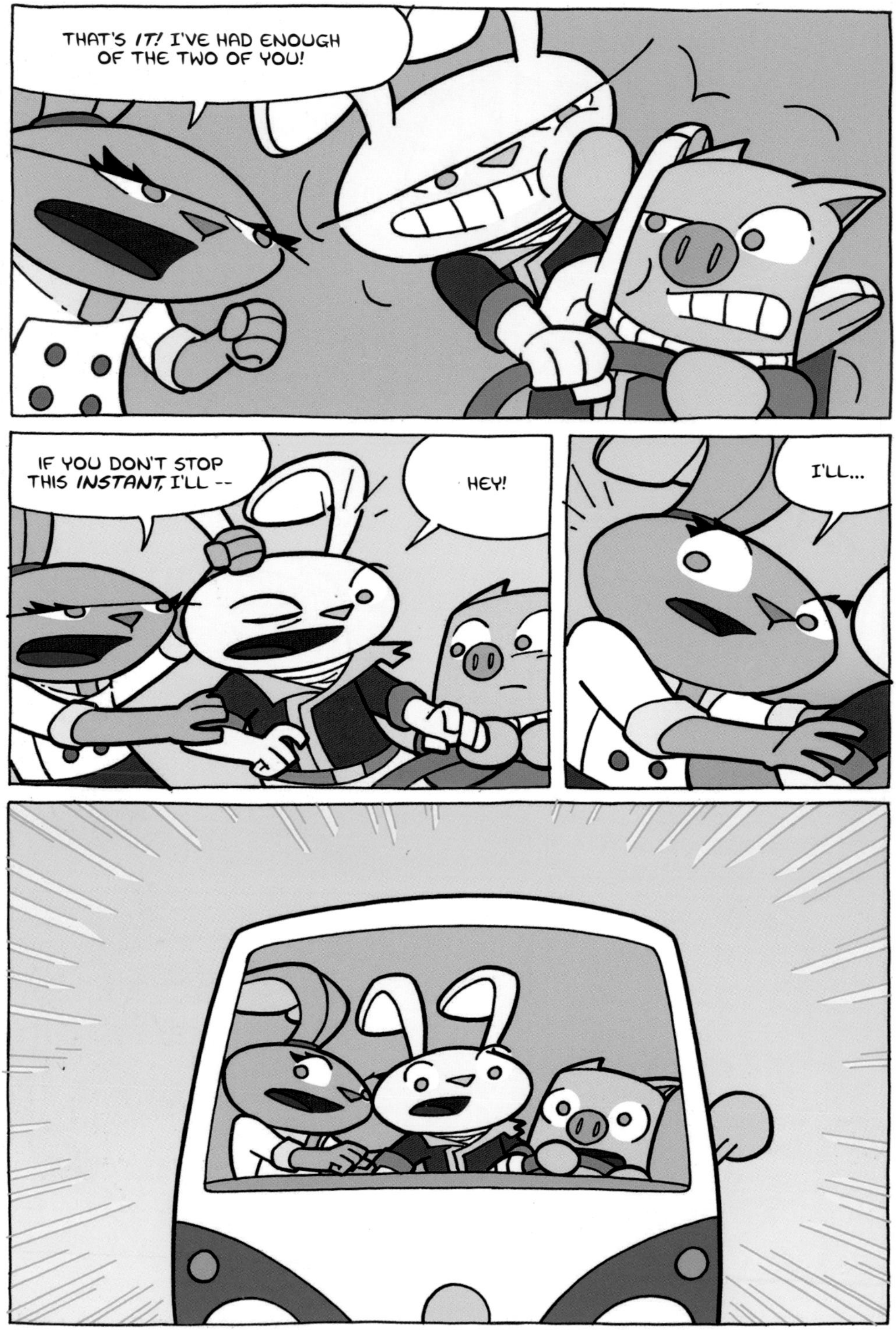

THAT'S *IT!* I'VE HAD ENOUGH OF THE TWO OF YOU!
IF YOU DON'T STOP THIS *INSTANT,* I'LL --
HEY!
I'LL...

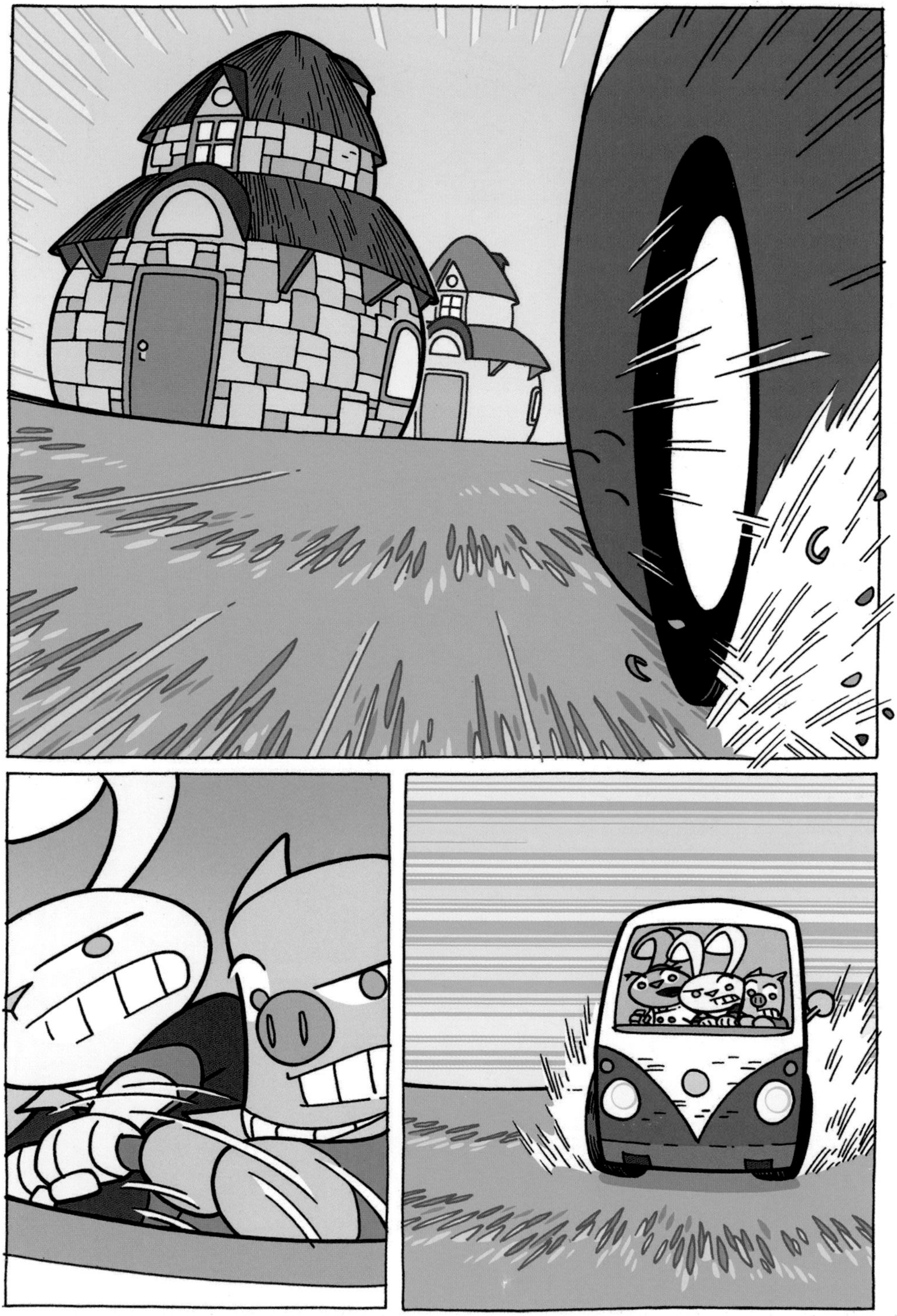

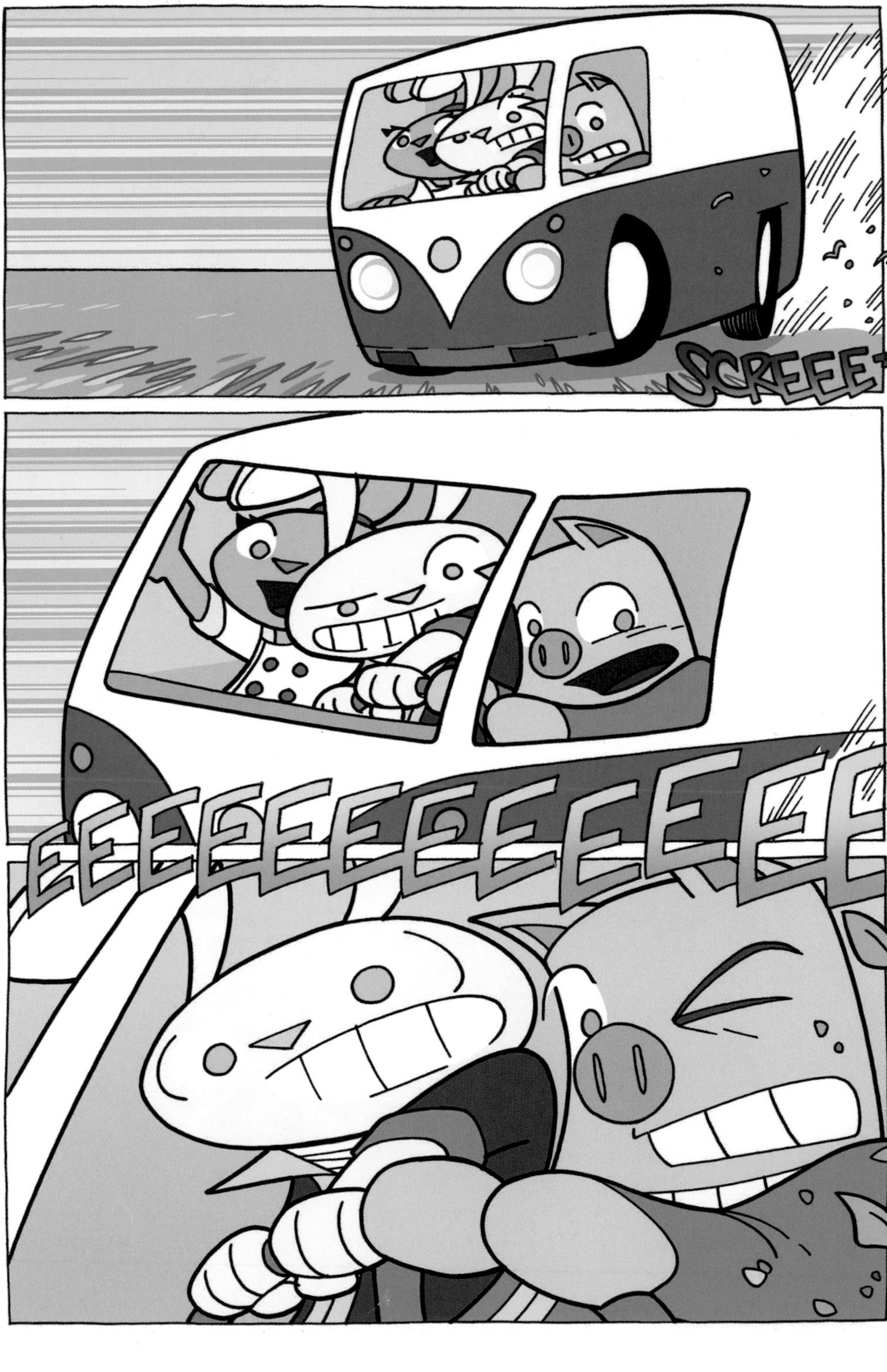
SCREEE-
EEEEEEEEEEEE

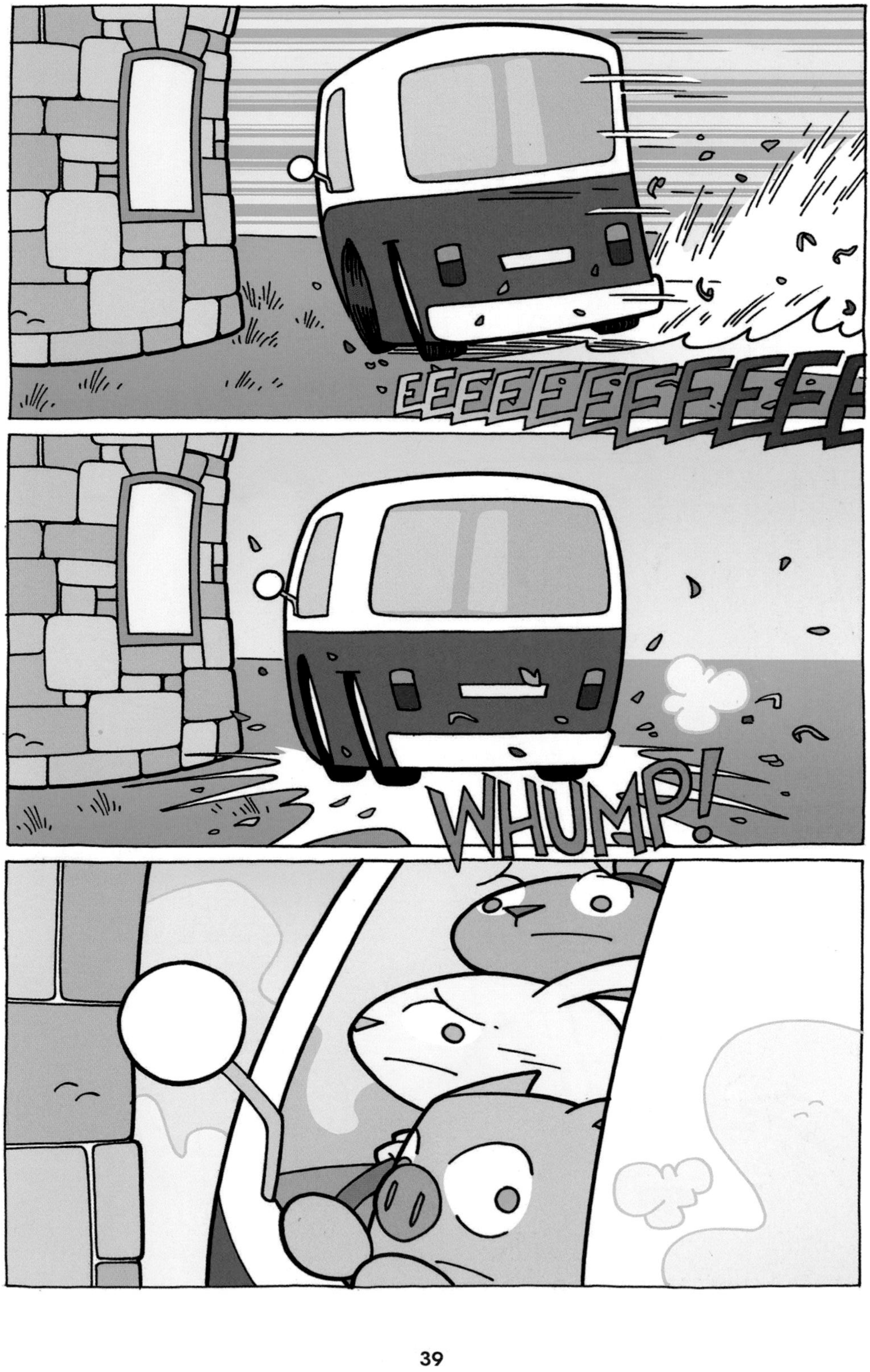
EEEEEEEEEEE
WHUMP!

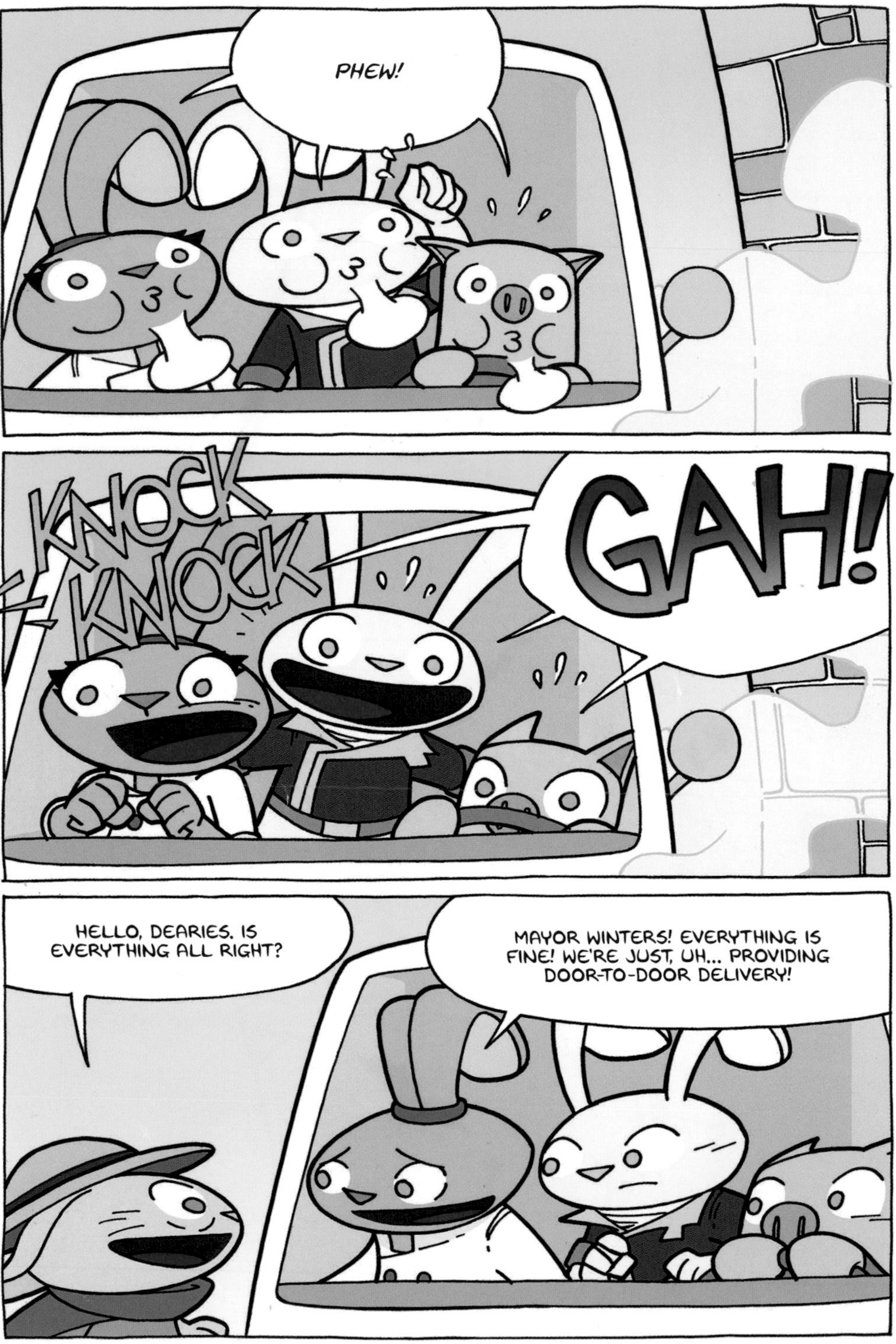
PHEW!
KNOCK KNOCK
GAH!
HELLO, DEARIES. IS EVERYTHING ALL RIGHT?
MAYOR WINTERS! EVERYTHING IS FINE! WE'RE JUST, UH... PROVIDING DOOR-TO-DOOR DELIVERY!

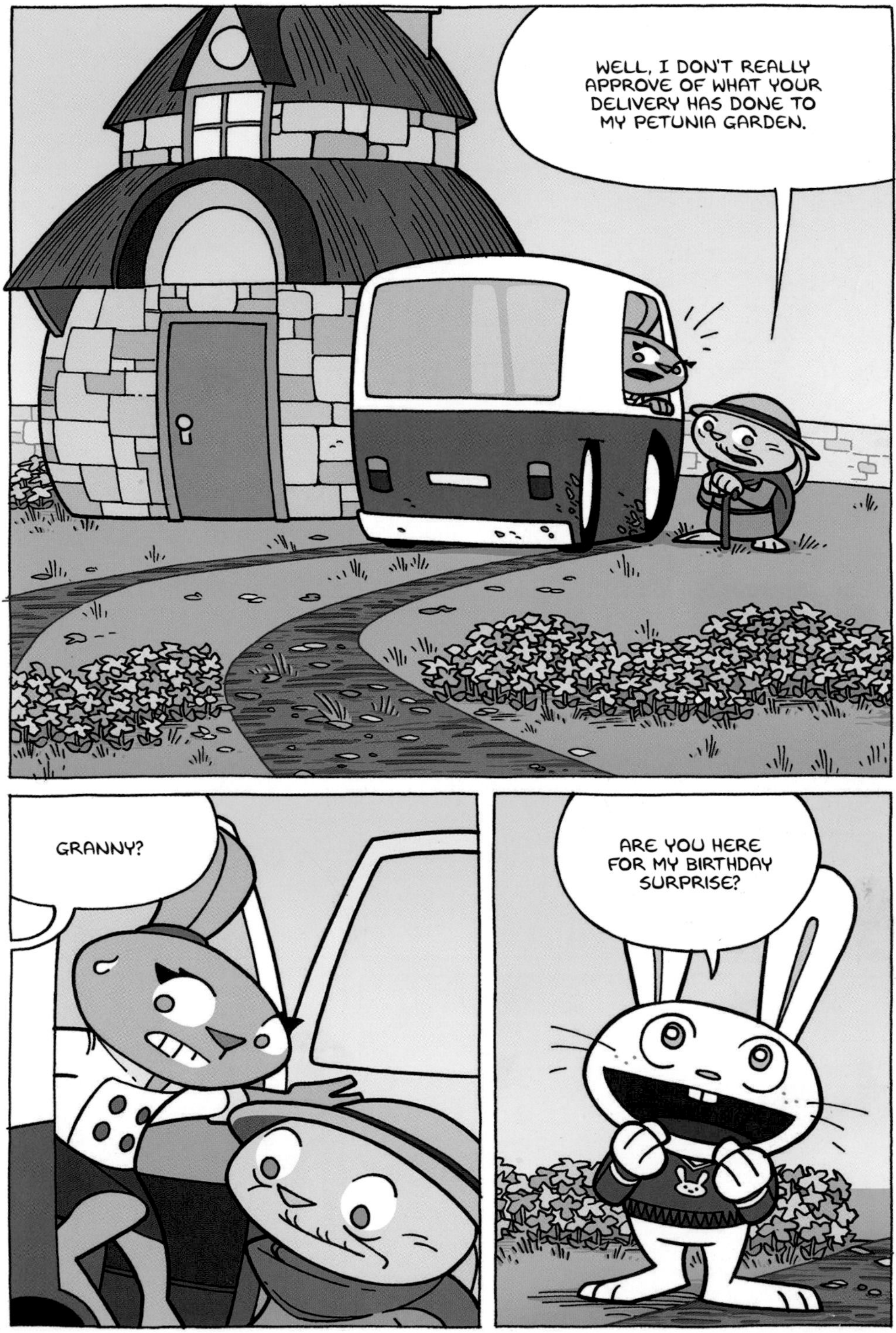
WELL, I DON'T REALLY APPROVE OF WHAT YOUR DELIVERY HAS DONE TO MY PETUNIA GARDEN.
GRANNY?
ARE YOU HERE FOR MY BIRTHDAY SURPRISE?

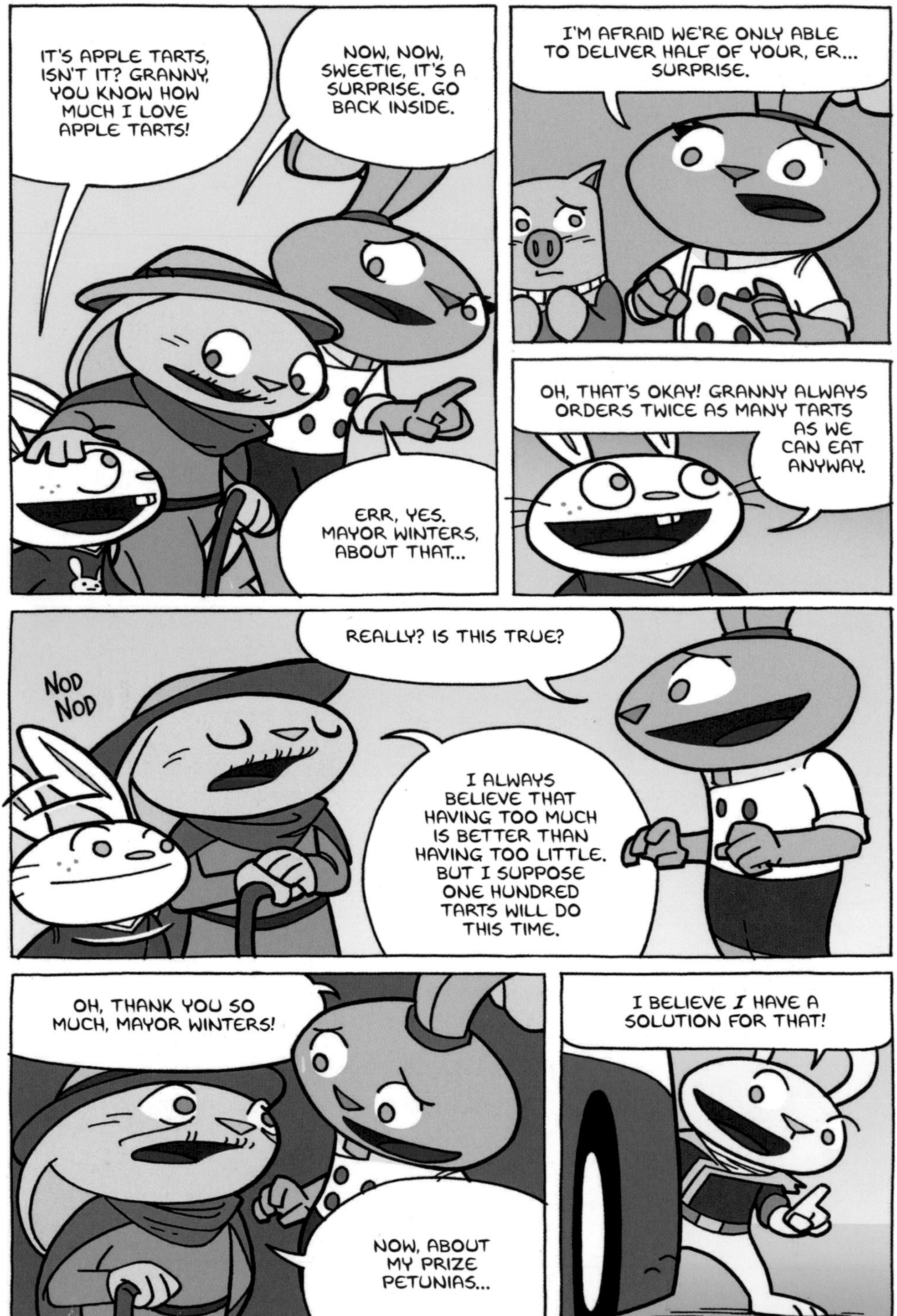
IT'S APPLE TARTS, ISN'T IT? GRANNY, YOU KNOW HOW MUCH I LOVE APPLE TARTS!
NOW, NOW, SWEETIE, IT'S A SURPRISE. GO BACK INSIDE.
ERR, YES. MAYOR WINTERS, ABOUT THAT...
I'M AFRAID WE'RE ONLY ABLE TO DELIVER HALF OF YOUR, ER... SURPRISE.
OH, THAT'S OKAY! GRANNY ALWAYS ORDERS TWICE AS MANY TARTS AS WE CAN EAT ANYWAY.
REALLY? IS THIS TRUE?
NOD NOD
I ALWAYS BELIEVE THAT HAVING TOO MUCH IS BETTER THAN HAVING TOO LITTLE. BUT I SUPPOSE ONE HUNDRED TARTS WILL DO THIS TIME.
OH, THANK YOU SO MUCH, MAYOR WINTERS!
NOW, ABOUT MY PRIZE PETUNIAS...
I BELIEVE I HAVE A SOLUTION FOR THAT!

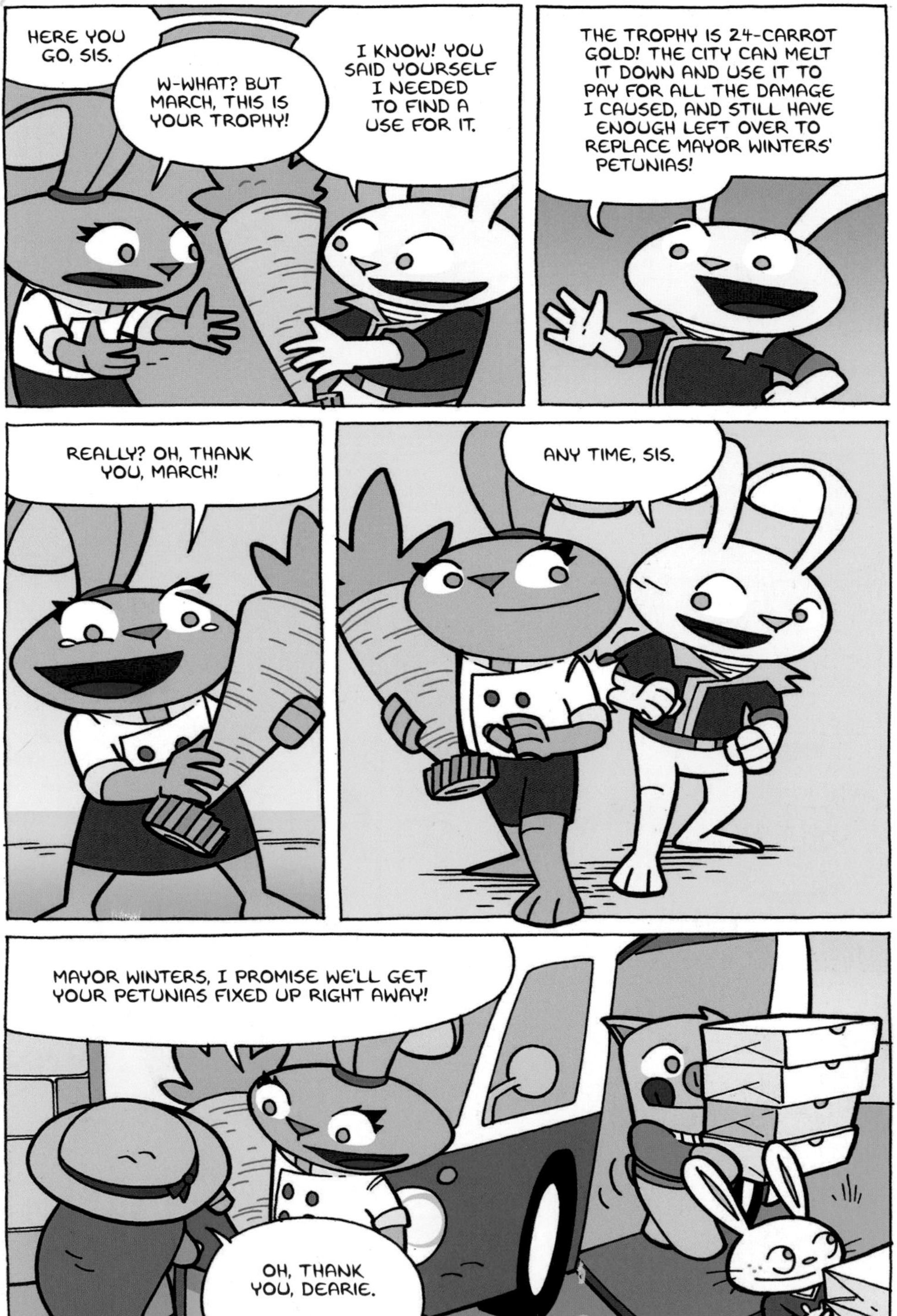
HERE YOU GO, SIS.
W-WHAT? BUT MARCH, THIS IS YOUR TROPHY!
I KNOW! YOU SAID YOURSELF I NEEDED TO FIND A USE FOR IT.
THE TROPHY IS 24-CARROT GOLD! THE CITY CAN MELT IT DOWN AND USE IT TO PAY FOR ALL THE DAMAGE I CAUSED, AND STILL HAVE ENOUGH LEFT OVER TO REPLACE MAYOR WINTERS' PETUNIAS!
REALLY? OH, THANK YOU, MARCH!
ANY TIME, SIS.
MAYOR WINTERS, I PROMISE WE'LL GET YOUR PETUNIAS FIXED UP RIGHT AWAY!
OH, THANK YOU, DEARIE.

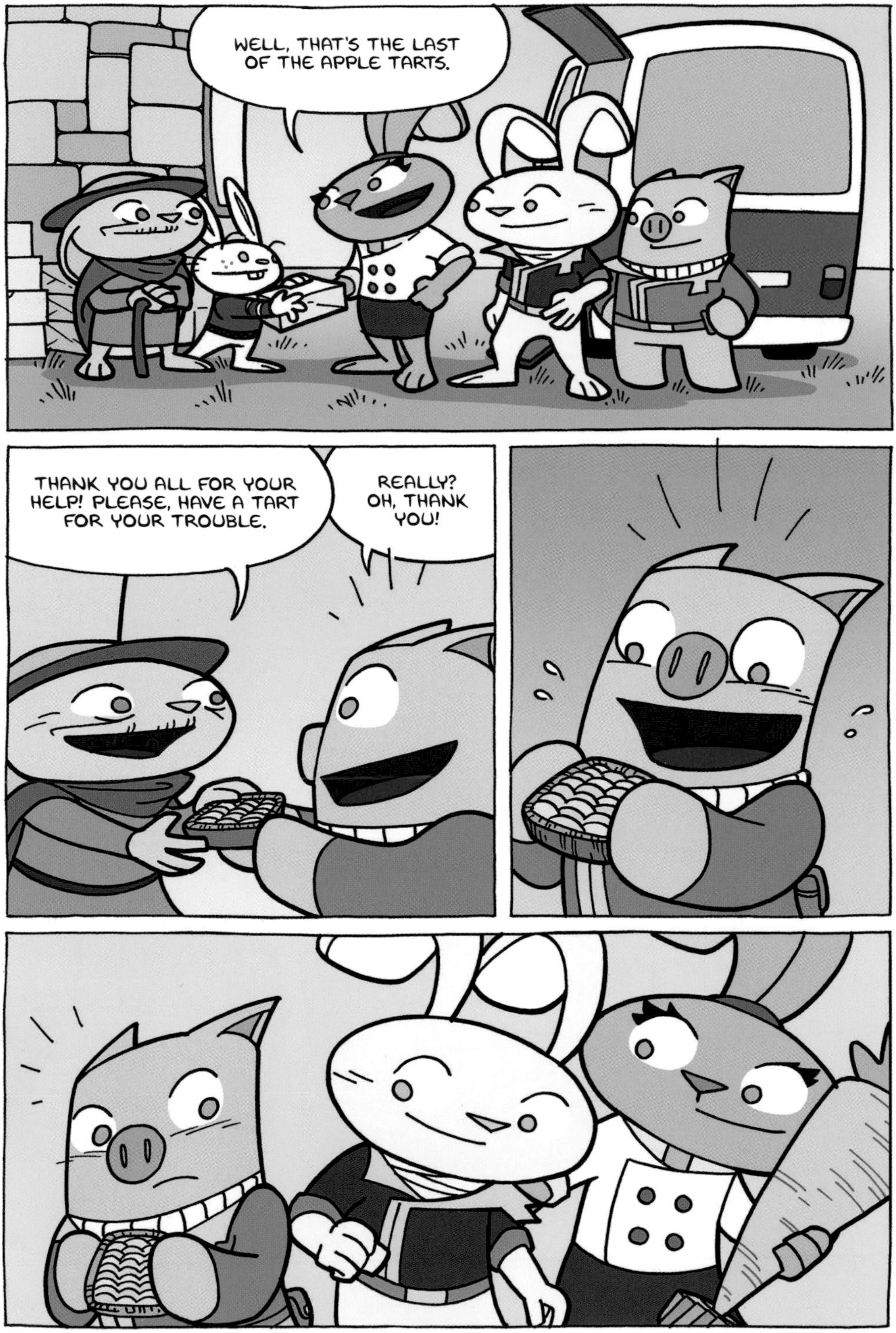
WELL, THAT'S THE LAST OF THE APPLE TARTS.
THANK YOU ALL FOR YOUR HELP! PLEASE, HAVE A TART FOR YOUR TROUBLE.
REALLY? OH, THANK YOU!

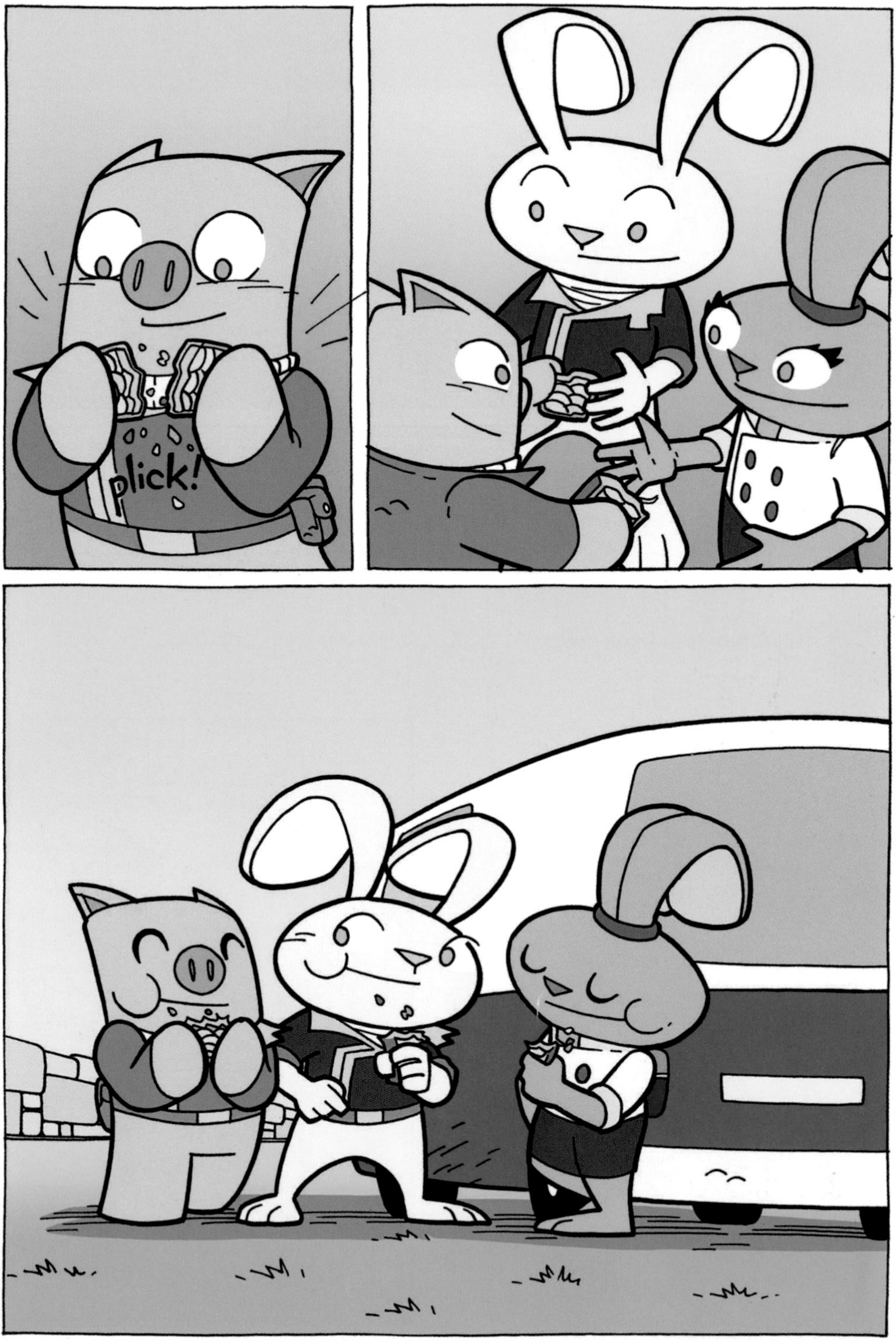
plick!

SKETCHES

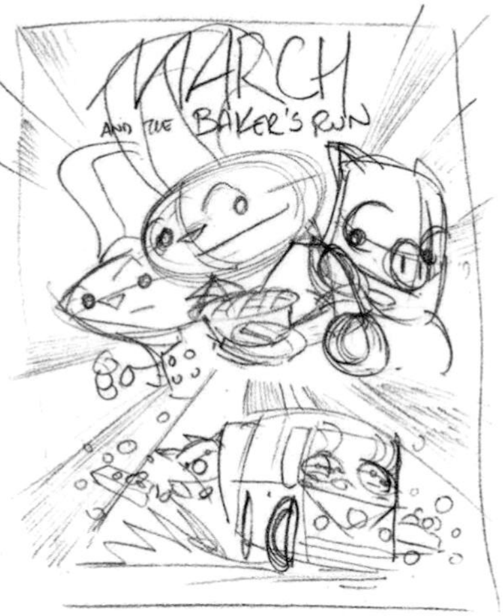
MARCH
AND THE BAKER'S RUN

1. Cover thumbnail rough

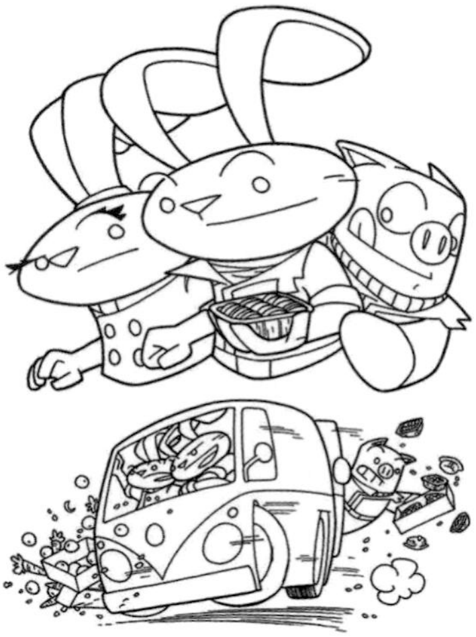

2. Inks

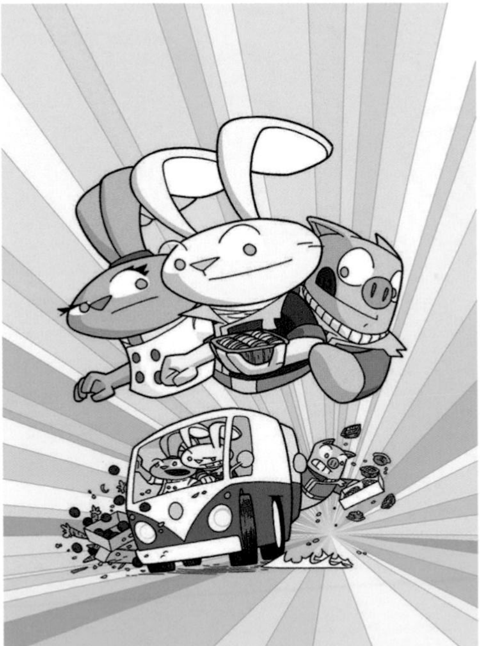

3. Colors & final corrections

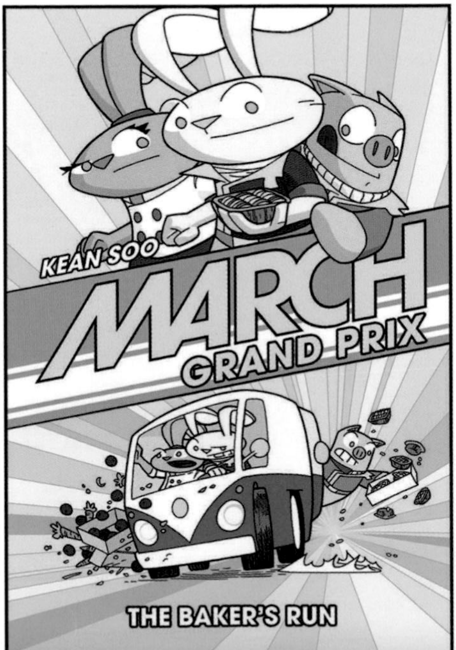
KEAN SOO
MARCH
GRAND PRIX
THE BAKER'S RUN

4. Final cover

New design sketches for The Baker's Run

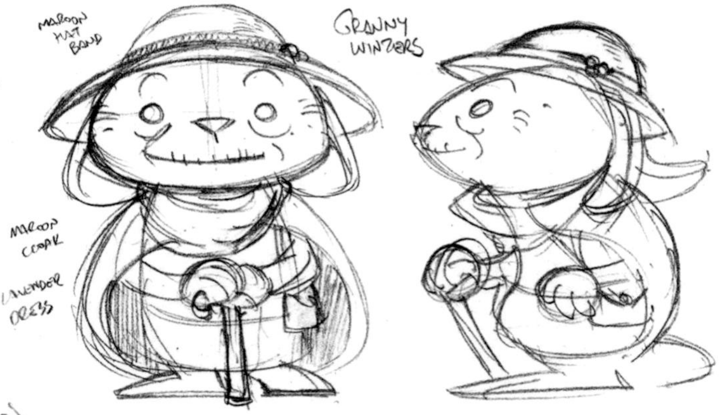
MAROON HAT BAND
MAROON CLOAK
LAVENDER DRESS

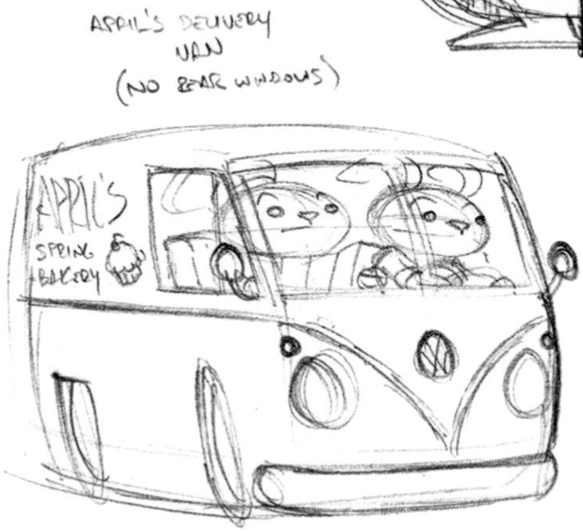
APRIL'S DELIVERY VAN (NO REAR WINDOWS)
APRIL'S
SPRING BAKERY

I will often draw a panel several times to find the most interesting staging for a scene. The series of studies below are all different variations of panel 3 on page 32.

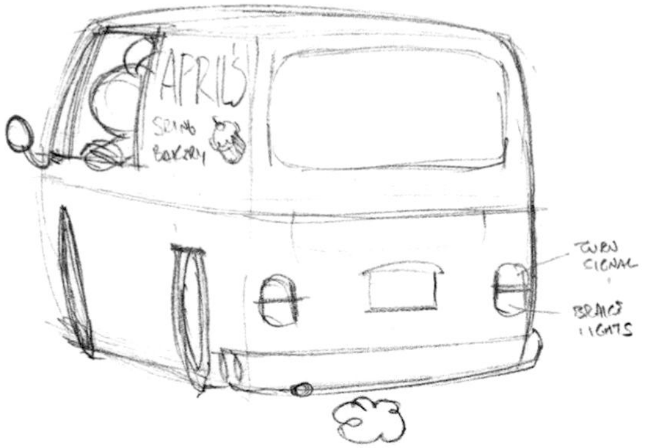
APRIL'S
SPRING BAKERY
TURN SIGNAL
BRAKE LIGHTS

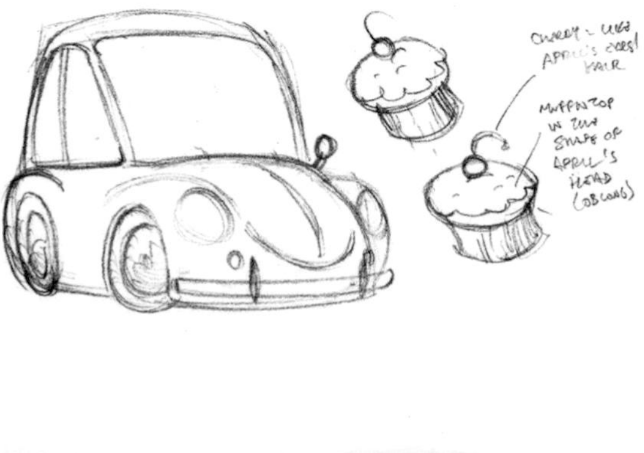
MUFFIN TOP IN THE SHAPE OF APRIL'S HEAD (OBLONG)

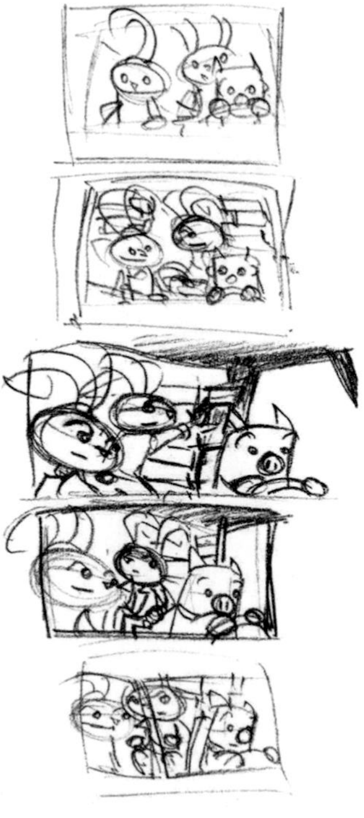

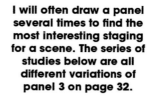

KEAN SOO

Kean Soo was born in the United Kingdom, grew up in various parts of Canada and Hong Kong, trained as an electrical engineer, and now draws comics for a living. A former assistant editor and contributor for the FLIGHT comics anthology, Kean also created the award-winning Jellaby series of graphic novels.

Kean currently lives in Toronto with his wife, their dog Reginald Barkley, and their 1992 Volvo 940 Turbo.

Kean would also like to thank Judy Hansen, Donnie Lemke, Brann Garvey, Tony Cliff, Kazu Kibuishi, everyone in the FLIGHT crew, and Tory Woollcott for making March Grand Prix such a joy to work on.

WITHDRAWN

3 1901 05419 8942